William H. G. Kingston

Adventures in the Far West

William H. G. Kingston

Adventures in the Far West

ISBN/EAN: 9783337178673

Printed in Europe, USA, Canada, Australia, Japan

Cover: Foto ©Andreas Hilbeck / pixelio.de

More available books at **www.hansebooks.com**

ADVENTURES

IN

THE FAR WEST.

IN

THE FAR WEST

BY

WILLIAM H. G. KINGSTON

AUTHOR OF "GREAT AFRICAN TRAVELLERS," "DIGBY HEATHCOTE,"
"SHIPWRECKS AND DISASTERS AT SEA," ETC.

WITH ILLUSTRATIONS

LONDON

GEORGE ROUTLEDGE AND SONS, LIMITED

BROADWAY, LUDGATE HILL

MANCHESTER AND NEW YORK

LONDON :
BRADBURY, AGNEW, & CO. LD., PRINTERS WHITEFRIARS.

LIST OF ILLUSTRATIONS.

ADVENTURES

IN

THE FAR WEST.

CHAPTER I.

"I SAY, didn't you hear a cry?" exclaimed Charley Fielding, starting up from the camp fire at which we were seated discussing our evening meal of venison, the result of our day's hunting. He leaned forward in the attitude of listening. "I'm sure I heard it! There it is again, but whether uttered by Redskin or four-footed beast is more than I can say."

We all listened, but our ears were not as sharp as Charley's, for we could hear nothing.

"Sit down, Charley, my boy, and finish your supper. It was probably fancy, or maybe the hoot of an owl to its mate," said our jovial companion, Dick Buntin, who never allowed any matter to disturb him, if he could help it, while engaged in stowing away his food.

Dick had been a lieutenant in the navy, and had knocked about the world in all climes, and seen no small amount of service. He had lately joined our party with Charley Fielding, a fatherless lad whom he had taken under his wing.

We, that is Jack Story and myself, Tom Rushforth, had come out from England together to the far west, to enjoy a few months' buffalo hunting, deer stalking, grisly and panther shooting, and beaver trapping, not to speak of the chances of an occasional brush with the Redskins, parties of whom were said to be on the war-path across the regions it was our intention to traverse, though none of us were inclined to be turned aside by the warnings we had received to that effect from our friends down east.

We had been pushing on further and further west, gaining experience, and becoming inured to the fatigues and dangers of a hunter's life. Having traversed Missouri and Kansas, though we had hitherto met with no adventures worthy of note, we had that evening pitched our camp in the neighbourhood of Smoky-hill fork, the waters of which, falling into the Arkansas, were destined ultimately to reach the far-off Mississippi.

We had furnished ourselves with a stout horse apiece, and four mules to carry our stores, consisting of salt pork, beans, biscuit, coffee, and a few other necessaries, besides our spare guns, ammunition, and the meat and skins of the animals we might kill.

Having, a little before sunset, fixed on a spot for our camp, with a stream on one side, and on the other a wood, which would afford us fuel and shelter from the keen night air which blew off the distant mountains, we had unsaddled and unpacked our horses and mules, the packs being placed so as to form a circular enclosure about eight paces in diameter.

Our first care had been to water and hobble our animals, and then to turn them loose to graze, when we considered ourselves at liberty to attend to our own wants. Having collected a quantity of dry sticks, we had lighted our fire in the centre of the circle, filled our water-kettle, and put on our meat to cook. Our next care had been to arrange our sleeping places. For this purpose we cut a quantity of willows which grew on the banks of the stream hard by, and we each formed a semi-circular hut, by sticking the extremities of the osier twigs into the ground, and bending them over so as to form a succession of arches. These were further secured by weaving a few flexible twigs along the top and sides of the framework, thus giving it sufficient stability to support the saddle-cloths and skins with which we covered them. By placing our buffalo-robes within, we had thus a comfortable and warm bed-place apiece, and were better protected from the fiercest storm raging without than we should have been inside a tent or ordinary hut.

Though this was our usual custom when materials were to be found, when not, we were content to wrap ourselves in our buffalo-robes, with our saddles for pillows.

All arrangements having been made, we sat down with keen appetites, our backs to our respective huts, to discuss the viands which had been cooking during the operations I have described. Dick Buntin, who generally performed the office of cook, had concocted a pot of coffee, having first roasted the berries in the lid of our saucepan, and then, wrapping them in a piece of deer-skin, had pounded them on a log with the head of a hatchet. Dick was about to serve out the smoking-hot coffee when Charley's exclamation made him stop to reply while he held the pot in his hand.

" I am sure I did hear a strange sound, and it was no owl's hoot, of that I am convinced," said Charley, still standing up, and peering out over the dark prairie. " Just keep silence for a few minutes, and you'll hear it too before long."

I listened, and almost directly afterwards a low mournful wail, wafted on the breeze, struck my ear. Dick and Story also acknowledged that they heard the sound.

" I knew I was not mistaken," said Charley; "what can it be?"

" An owl, or some other night-bird, as I at first thought," said Buntin. " Come, hand me your mugs, or I shall have to boil up the coffee again."

Charley resumed his seat, and we continued the pleasant occupation in which we were engaged. Supper over, we crept into our sleeping-places, leaving our fire blazing, not having considered it necessary as yet to keep watch at night.

We were generally, directly after we had stretched ourselves on the ground, fast asleep, for we rose at break of day, and sometimes even before it; but ere I had closed my eyes, I again heard, apparently coming from far off, the same sound which had attracted Charley's notice. It appeared to me more like the howl of a wolf than the cry of a night-bird, but I was too sleepy to pay any attention to it.

How long I had been in a state of unconsciousness I could not tell, when I was aroused by a chorus of howls and yelps, and, starting up, I saw a number of animals with glaring eyes almost in our very midst.

" Wolves, wolves! " I cried, calling to my companions at the top of my voice.

Before I could draw my rifle out of the hut, where I had placed it by my side, one of the brutes had seized on a large piece of venison, suspended at the end of a stick to keep it off the ground, and had darted off with it, while the depredators were searching round for other articles into which they could fix their fangs.

Our appearance greatly disconcerted them, as we shouted in chorus, and turning tail they began to decamp as fast as their legs would carry them.

" Bring down that fellow with the venison," I cried out.

Charley, who had been most on the alert, had his rifle ready, and, firing, brought down the thief. Another of the pack instantly seized the meat and made off with it in spite of the shouts we sent after him. The wolves lost three of their number, but the rest got off with the venison in triumph. It was a lesson to us to keep a watch at night, and more carefully to secure our venison. We had, however, a portion remaining to serve us for breakfast next morning.

We took good care not to let the wolves get into our camp again, but we heard the brutes howling around and quarrelling over the carcase of one of their companions, who had been shot but had not immediately dropped. Having driven off our unwelcome visitors, Charley and I went in search of our horses, as we were afraid they might have been attacked. They were, however, well able to take care of themselves and had made their way to the border of the stream, where we found them safe.

In the meantime Buntin and Story dragged the carcases of the wolves we had killed to a distance from the camp, as their skins were not worth preserving. We all then met round the camp fire, but we soon found that to sleep was impossible, for the wolves, having despatched their wounded companions, came back to feast on the others we had shot. We might have killed numbers while so employed, but that would have only detained them longer in our neighbourhood, and we hoped when they had picked the bones of their friends, that they would go away and leave us in peace.

We all wished to be off as soon as possible, so while it was still dark we caught and watered our horses; and, having cast off their hobbles and loaded the pack animals, we were in the saddle by sunrise. We rode on for several hours, and then encamped for breakfast, allowing our horses to graze while we went on foot in search of game. We succeeded in killing a couple of deer and a turkey, so that we were again amply supplied with food. Our baggage-mules being slow but sure-going animals we were unable to make more than twenty miles a day, though at a pinch we could accomplish thirty. We had again mounted and were moving forward. The country was covered with tall

AN ENCOUNTER WITH WOLVES

grass, five and sometimes eight feet in height, over which we could scarcely look even when on horseback. We had ridden about a couple of miles from our last camping-place, when Story, the tallest of our party, exclaimed—

" I see some objects moving to the northward. They look to me like mounted men, and are apparently coming in this direction."

He unslung his glass, while we all pulled up and took a look in the direction he pointed.

"Yes, I thought so," he exclaimed; "they are Indians, though, as there are not many of them, they are not likely to attack us; but we must be on our guard, notwithstanding."

We consulted what was best to be done.

" Ride steadily in the direction we are going," said Dick; "and, by showing that we are not afraid of them, when they see our rifles they will probably sheer off, whatever may be their present intentions. But keep together, my lads, and let nothing tempt us to separate."

We followed Dick's advice; indeed, although we had no ostensible leader, he always took the post on an emergency.

The strangers approached, moving considerably faster than we were doing. As they drew nearer, Story, who took another view of them through his glass, announced that there were two white men of the party, thus dispelling all fears we might have entertained of an encounter. We therefore pulled up to wait their arrival. As they got still nearer to us, one of the white men rode forward. He was followed by several dogs. Suddenly Dick, who had been regarding him attentively, exclaimed—

" What, Harry Armitage, my dear fellow! What has brought you here ? "

"A question much easier asked than answered, and I'll put the same to you," said the stranger, shaking hands.

"I came out for a change of scene, and to get further from the ocean than I have ever before been in my life; and now let me introduce you to my friends," said Dick.

The usual forms were gone through. Mr. Armitage then introduced his companion as Pierre Buffet, one of the best hunters and trappers throughout the continent. The Indians, he said, had been engaged by Pierre and himself to act as guides and scouts, and to take care of the horses and baggage-mules. As our objects were the same, before we had ridden very far we agreed to continue together, as we should thus, in passing through territories infested by hostile Indians, be the better able to defend ourselves.

We had reason, before long, to be thankful that our party had thus been strengthened. We encamped as usual; and, not forgetting the lesson we had lately received, we set a watch so that we should not be surprised, either by wolves or Redskins. Though the former were heard howling in the distance, we were not otherwise disturbed by them, and at dawn we were once more in our saddles traversing the wide extending prairie, our new associates and we exchanging accounts of the various adventures we had met with. Armitage was not very talkative, but Dick managed to draw him out more than could any of the rest of the party. Buffet, in his broken English, talked away sufficiently to make ample amends for his employer's taciturnity. Our midday halt was over, and we did not again intend to encamp until nightfall, at a spot described by Buffet on the banks of a stream which ran round a rocky height on the borders of the prairie. It was, however, some distance off, and we did not expect to reach it until later in the day than usual.

We were riding on, when I saw one of the Indians standing up in his stirrups and looking to the north-east. Presently he called to Buntin and pointed in the same direction. The words uttered were such as to cause us no little anxiety. The prairie was on fire. The sharp eyes of the Indian had distinguished the wreaths of smoke which rose above the tall grass, and which I should have taken for a thick mist or cloud gathering in the horizon. The wind blew from the same quarter.

" Messieurs, we must put our horses to their best speed," exclaimed Pierre. " If the wind gets up, that fire will come on faster than we can go, and we shall all be burnt into cinders if once overtaken."

" How far off is it ?" asked Dick.

" Maybe eight or ten miles, but that is as nothing. It will travel five or six miles in the hour, even with this wind blowing—and twice as fast before a gale. On, on, messieurs, there is no time to talk about the matter, for between us and where the flames now rage, there is nothing to stop their progress."

We needed no further urging, but driving on the mules with shouts and blows—as we had no wish to abandon them if it could be avoided—we dashed on.

c

Every now and then I looked back to observe the progress of the conflagration. Dark wreaths were rising higher and higher in the sky, and below them forked flames ever and anon darted up as the fire caught the more combustible vegetation. Borne by the wind, light powdery ashes fell around us, while we were sensible of a strong odour of burning, which made it appear as if the enemy was already close at our heels. The grass on every side was too tall and dry to enable us—as is frequently done under such circumstances, by setting fire to the herbage—to clear a space in which we could remain while the conflagration passed by.

Our only chance of escaping was by pushing forward. On neither side did Pierre or the Indians know of any spot where we could take refuge nearer than the one ahead. Every instant the smoke grew thicker, and we could hear the roaring, crackling, rushing sound of the flames, though still, happily for us, far away. Prairie-hens, owls, and other birds would flit by, presently followed by numerous deer and buffalo; while whole packs of wolves rushed on regardless of each other and of us, prompted by instinct to make their escape from the apprehended danger. Now a bear who had been foraging on the plain ran by, eager to seek his mountain home; and I caught sight of two or more panthers springing over the ground at a speed which would secure their safety. Here and there small game scampered along, frequently meeting the death they were trying to avoid, from the feet of the larger animals; snakes went wriggling among the grass, owls hooted, wolves yelped, and other animals added their cries to the terror-prompted chorus. Our chance of escaping with our baggage-mules seemed small indeed. The hot air struck our cheeks, as we turned round every now and then to see how near the fire had approached. The dogs kept up bravely at the feet of their masters' horse.

" If we are to save our own skins, we must abandon our mules," cried out Dick Buntin in a voice such as that with which he was wont to hail the main-top.

" No help for it, I fear," answered Armitage; "what do you say, Pierre?"

" Let the beasts go. *Sauve qui peut !*" answered the Canadian.

There was no time to stop and unload the poor brutes. To have done so would have afforded them a better chance of preserving their lives, though we must still lose our luggage.

The word was given, the halters by which we had been dragging the animals on were cast off; and, putting spurs into the flanks of our steeds, we galloped forward. Our horses seemed to know their danger as well as we did. I was just thinking of the serious consequences of a fall, when down came Dick, who was leading just ahead of me with Charley by his side. His horse had put its foot into a prairie-dog's hole.

" Are you hurt?" I cried out.

" No, no; go on; don't wait for me," he answered. But neither Charley nor I was inclined to do that.

Dick was soon on his feet again, while we assisted him. in spite of what he had said, to get up his horse.

The animal's leg did not appear to be strained, and
Dick quickly again climbed into the saddle.

" Thank you, my dear boys," he exclaimed, " it
must not happen again ; I am a heavy weight for my
brute, and, if he comes down, you must go on and let
me shift for myself."

We made no reply, for neither Charley nor I was
inclined to desert our brave friend. The rest of the
party had dashed by, scarcely observing what had
taken place, the Indians taking the lead. It was
impossible to calculate how many miles we had gone.
Night was coming on, making the glare to the eastward appear brighter and more terrific. The mules
were still instinctively following us, but we were
distancing them fast, though we could distinguish
their shrieks of terror amid the general uproar.

The hill for which we were making rose up before
us, covered, as it appeared, by shrubs and grasses.
It seemed doubtful whether it would afford us the
safety we sought. We could scarcely hope that our
horses would carry us beyond it, for already they
were giving signs of becoming exhausted. We
might be preserved by taking up a position in the
centre of the stream, should it be sufficiently shallow
to enable us to stand in it ; but that was on the other
side of the hill, and the fire might surround us before
we could gain its banks. We could barely see the
dark outline of the hill ahead, the darkness being increased by the contrast of the lurid flames raging
behind us. We dashed across the more open space,
where the grass was for some reason of less height
than in other parts. Here many of the animals

which had passed us, paralyzed by fear, had halted
as if expecting that they would be safe from the
flames. Deer and wolves, bison, and even a huge
bear—not a grizzly, however—and many smaller
creatures were lying down or running round and
round.

I thought Pierre would advise our stopping here,
but he shouted, "On, on! This is no place for us;
de beasts soon get up and run away too!"

We accordingly dashed forward, but every moment
the heat and smell of the fire was increasing. The
smoke, which blew around us in thick wreaths driven
by the wind, was almost overpowering. This made
the conflagration appear even nearer than it really
was. At length, Pierre shouted out :

"Dis way, messieurs, dis way!" and I found that
we had reached the foot of a rocky hill which rose
abruptly out of the plain. He led us round its base
until we arrived at a part up which we could manage
to drag our horses. Still it seemed very doubtful if
we should be safe, for grass covered the lower parts,
and, as far as I could judge, shrubs and trees the
upper : still there was nothing else to be done.
Throwing ourselves from our horses, we continued to
drag them up the height, Pierre's shouts guiding us.
I was the last but one, Dick insisting on taking the
post of danger in the rear and sending Charley and
me before him. The horses were as eager to get up
as we were, their instinct showing them that safety
was to be found near human beings. Our only fear
was that the other animals would follow, and that we
should have more companions than we desired. The

top was soon gained, when we lost no time in setting
to work to clear a space in which we could remain,
by cutting down the grass immediately surrounding
us, and then firing the rest on the side of the hill towards which the conflagration was approaching. We
next beat down the flames we had kindled, with our
blankets—a hot occupation during which we were
nearly smothered by the smoke rushing in our faces.
The fire burnt but slowly against the wind, which
was so far an advantage.

"We are safe now, messieurs!" exclaimed Pierre
at last; and we all, in one sense, began to breathe
more freely, although the feeling of suffocation from
the smoke was trying in the extreme.

We could now watch, more calmly than before, the
progress of the fire as it rushed across the country,
stretching far on either side of us, and lighting up the
hills to the north and south, and the groves which
grew near them. We often speak of the scarlet line
of the British troops advancing on the foe, and such
in appearance was the fire; for we could see it from
the heights where we stood, forming a line of a width
which it seemed possible to leap over, or at all events
to dash through without injury. Now it divided, as
it passed some rocky spot or marshy ground. Now
it again united, and the flames were seen licking up
the grass which they had previously spared.

Our poor baggage-animals caused us much anxiety.
Had they escaped or fallen victims to the flames with
our property, and the most valuable portion of it—
the ammunition? Charley declared that he heard
some ominous reports, and the Indians nodded as

THE PRAIRIE ON FIRE.

they listened to what he said, and made signs to signify that the baggage had been blown up. For some minutes we were surrounded by a sea of flame, and had to employ ourselves actively in rushing here and there and extinguishing the portions which advanced close upon us, our horses in the meantime standing perfectly still and trembling in every limb, fully alive to their dangerous position. At length, after a few anxious hours, the fire began to die out; but here we were on the top of a rock, without food or water, and with only so much powder and shot as each man carried in his pouch. Still, we had saved our lives and our horses, and had reason to be thankful. The spot was a bleak one to camp in, but we had no choice. To protect ourselves from the wind, we built up a hedge of brushwood, and lighted a fire. Food we could not hope to obtain until the morning, but Pierre and one of the Indians volunteered to go down to the river, and to bring some water in a leathern bottle which the Canadian carried at his saddle-bow. He had also saved a tin cup, but the whole of our camp equipage had shared the fate of the mules, whatever that might be. The sky was overcast, and, as we looked out from our height over the prairie, one vast mass of blackness alone could be seen.

After quenching the thirst produced by the smoke and heat with the water brought by Pierre and his companion, we lay down to sleep.

At daylight we were on foot. The first thing to be done was to ascertain the fate of the mules, and the next to obtain some game to satisfy the cravings of hunger. Pierre and the Indians descended into the plain for both purposes. Charley and I started off in one direction, and Armitage and Story in another, with our guns, along the rocky heights which extended away to the northward, while Dick volunteered to look after the horses and keep our fire burning.

We went on for some distance without falling in with any large game, and we were unwilling to expend our powder on small birds. Charley at last proposed that we should descend into the plain in the hopes of finding some animals killed by the fire.

" Very little chance of that," I remarked, "for by this time the wolves have eaten them up. We are more likely, if we keep on, to fall in with deer on the opposite side, where the fire has not reached."

We accordingly crossed the ridge, and were making our way to the westward, when we heard Armitage's dog giving tongue in the distance.

" They have found deer, at all events, and perhaps we may be in time to pick off one or two of the herd," I exclaimed.

We scrambled along over the rocks, until we reached the brink of a low precipice, looking over which we caught sight of a magnificent buck with a single dog at his heels. Just then the stag stopped, and, wheeling suddenly round, faced its pursuer. Near was a small pool which served to protect the stag from the attack of the hound in the rear. It appeared to us that it would have gone hard with the dog, for at any moment the antlers of the stag might have pinned it to the ground. We concluded, from not hearing the other dogs, that they had gone off in

a different direction, leaving this bold fellow—Lion,
by name—to follow his chase alone.

We crept along the rocks, keeping ourselves concealed until we had got near enough to take a steady
aim at the stag. I agreed to fire first, and, should I
miss, Charley was to try his skill. In the meantime
the dog kept advancing and retreating, seeking for an
opportunity to fly at the stag's throat; but even then,
should he succeed in fixing his fangs in the animal,
he would run great risk of being knelt upon. The
deer was as watchful as the dog, and the moment the
latter approached, down again went its formidable
antlers. Fearing that the deer might by some chance
escape, taking a steady aim I fired. To my delight,
over it rolled, when we both sprang down the rocks
and ran towards it.

While I reloaded, Charley, having beaten off the
dog, examined the deer to ascertain that it was really
dead. We then set to work to cut up our prize, intending to carry back the best portions to the camp.

While thus employed, we heard a shout and saw
our companions approaching with their dogs. They
had missed the remainder of the herd, and were too
happy in any way to obtain the deer to be jealous of
our success.

Laden with the meat, the whole of which we carried
with us, we returned to the camp, where we found
Dick ready with spits for roasting it. In a short time
Pierre and the Indians returned with the report that
they had found the mules dead, and already almost
devoured by the cayotes, while their cargoes had been
blown up, as we feared would be the case, with the

AT BAY.

powder they contained. They brought the spare. guns—the stocks of which, however, were sadly damaged by the fire. Our camp equipage, which was very welcome, was uninjured, together with a few knives and other articles of iron.

So serious was our loss, that it became absolutely necessary to return to the nearest settlement to obtain fresh pack-animals and a supply of powder.

CHAPTER II.

By the loss of our baggage, we were reduced to hard fare. We had no coffee, no corn meal, no salt or pepper; but our greatest want was powder. Should the ammunition in our pouches hold out, we hoped to obtain food enough to keep us from starving till we could reach the nearest settlement of Tillydrone. Before commencing our return journey, however, it would be necessary, we agreed, to obtain a supply of meat, as we should find but little game in the region we had to cross. We must push on through it, therefore, as fast as our horses could carry us; but after their hard gallop on the previous day, it would be necessary to give them several hours rest, and it was settled that we should remain encamped where we were until the following morning. The locality had many advantages: it was high and dry, while, commanding as it did an extensive view over the prairie, we could see any hostile Indians approaching, and could defend ourselves should they venture to attack us.

As soon as breakfast was over, and we had rested from the fatigues of the morning, we again set out on foot with our guns. Charley and I, as before, kept together. The rest divided into two parties, each hoping to add a good supply of meat to the common stock. We had entered into an agreement not to fire a shot, unless sure of our aim, as every charge, to us, was worth its weight in gold. A spot had been fixed on, where we were to meet, about a couple of miles from the camp, in the centre of the ridge. Charley and I had gone on for an hour or more, but had met with no game, when what was our delight to see a herd of a dozen large deer feeding in a glade below us ; and, although too far off to risk a shot, we hoped that by making a wide circuit we should be able to creep up to them on the lee side.

Taking the proposed direction, we observed a large clump of rose-bushes, which grew in great profusion in that region. Near them also were two or three trees, behind which we expected to be able to conceal ourselves while we took aim at the deer. Keeping as much under cover as possible, we reached the rose-bushes, when we began to creep along on hands and knees, trailing our guns after us. To our delight we found that the deer were still feeding quietly, un-suspicious of danger. I managed to reach one of the trees, Charley another. The two nearest animals were a stag and a doe. I agreed to shoot the former, Charley the latter.

He waited until I gave the signal, when our guns went off at the same instant. As the smoke cleared away, we saw that both our shot had taken effect. It had been settled that, in case the animals should at-tempt to get up, we were to rush out and despatch them with our hunting-knives. I ran towards the stag, which made an effort to escape, but rolled over

A SHOT IN TIME.

[/ 33.

and died just as I reached it. Turning round to ascertain how it fared with Charley, I saw the doe rise to her feet, though bleeding from a wound in the neck. I instantly reloaded to be ready to fire, knowing that under such circumstances even a doe might prove a dangerous antagonist. It was fortunate that I did so, for the animal, throwing herself upon her haunches, began to strike out fiercely with her fore-feet, a blow from which would have fractured my friend's skull. Seeing his hat fall to the ground, I was afraid that he had been struck. Holding his rifle, which he had unfortunately forgotten to reload, before him in the fashion of a single-stick, he attempted to defend himself; but one of the animal's hoofs, striking his shoulder, brought him to the ground, so that he was unable to spring back out of harm's way. For a moment the deer retreated, but then again came on with her fore-feet in the air, intent on mischief. Now was the moment to fire, as the next Charley might be struck lifeless to the ground. I pulled the trigger, aiming at the head of the doe ; for, had I attempted to shoot her in the breast, I might have hit my companion. As the smoke cleared away I saw the deer spring into the air and fall lifeless to the ground. The bullet had struck her in the very spot I intended. Charley rose to his feet, and I ran forward, anxious to ascertain if he was injured. Providentially, his ramrod alone was broken, and, except a bruise on the shoulder which caused him some pain, he had escaped without damage.

We lost no time in skinning and cutting up the deer, which having done, we formed two packages of as much of the meat as we could carry, while we suspended the remainder to the bough of a neighbouring tree, to return for it before night-fall. Our companions were nearly as successful, each party having killed a deer, the whole of which they brought into camp. We left them all employed in cutting the chief portion into strips to dry in the sun, so that it could be transported more easily than in a fresh state. As we approached the spot where we had left the venison, a loud yelping which reached our ears told us that the cayotes had found it out. The brutes were not worth powder and shot, so getting some thick sticks, we rushed in among them and drove them off to a distance. They returned, however, as soon as we had got down the venison and were employed in packing it up, and we had to make several onslaughts, during which we killed three or four of the wolves, who were instantly devoured by their companions. While they were thus employed, we had time to pack up our game, but the rapacious creatures followed howling at our heels until we reached the camp. All night long also they continued their unpleasant chorus.

In the morning, having breakfasted on fresh venison, we started, each man carrying a load of the dried meat. Our object was to push on as fast as possible, only halting when necessary to rest our horses, or to kill some buffalo or deer, should any be seen. Pierre especially advised that we should otherwise make no delay, saying that he had observed the trails of Indians, who were probably out on the war-path, and that, at all events, it would be necessary to be on our guard against them.

We crossed the burnt prairie, our horses' hoofs stirring up the ashes as we scampered along. Frequently we came upon the bodies of small animals which had failed to escape from the fire. We saw also numbers of snakes, some burnt to death, others only scorched and still managing to make their way over the ground. We were thankful when, having crossed a stream, we got into a more cheerful tract of country. Here Pierre advised that we should bo doubly on our guard, as in all probability the Indians themselves had fired the grass, either to burn us, or to deprive us of our beasts of burden, as they succeeded in doing, that we might the more easily fall into their hands, but that such was the case it was difficult to say. Perhaps, when they found us strongly posted, they had considered it prudent not to attack us.

We had started before day-break, and proposed halting for a couple of hours to breakfast and rest our beasts, when, just as the rich glow which ushers in the rising sun had suffused the sky, one of the Indians, addressing Pierre, pointed to the south-west.

" What is it he says?" I asked.

" Indians!" answered Pierre, "on foot and on horseback, a 1 d no small number of them. We must 'be prepared for them, messieurs; for, if I mistake not, they are Coomanches, and they are difficult customers to deal with in the open. If we were within a stockade, we should quickly send them to the right about, though, as they stand in awe of our rifles, it is a question whether they will attack us as long as we show a bold front."

" It is of little use to show a bold front in the centre of a wild prairie, with a hundred howling savages galloping about one," I thought to myself.

However, none of our party were men to flinch. By Pierre's advice we rode steadily forward. There was a slight elevation at some distance, with a small lake beyond it. Buntin, who took the lead, proposed that we should try to gain it, as it would give us an advantage over our nimble foes, as, while they were ascending its steep sides, we could shoot them down without difficulty. On we rode therefore as fast as we could venture to go, for it was important not to blow our horses, lest we should have to come to an encounter with the Redskins.

We had got to within a quarter of a mile or so from the height, when we saw that the Indians had divined our intention, a party of them, who must have made a wide circuit, having already taken possession of it.

" Never mind, boys," said Dick in a cheery voice —" we can fight them if they are in a fighting mood just as well on the plains as on the top of yonder hill. They probably think that all our powder is lost, and expect to gain an easy victory."

" It will be wise to dismount, messieurs," said Pierre. " Each man must take post behind his horse, and when the savages come on we must wait until they get near enough to afford us a sure mark."

" We will follow Pierre's advice," said Dick, "but we will wait to ascertain whether they have hostile intentions or not. Our best plan is to proceed steadily on as if we were not conscious of their presence."

THE INDIAN FLYING-SHOTS.

We continued, therefore, riding forward, so as to pass the hill about the eighth of a mile on our right, keeping a careful watch on the Redskins. Suddenly there was a movement among them, and out dashed several horsemen. Sweeping around the hill, they approached us. We lost not a moment, and, placing ourselves as arranged, we stood with our rifles ready to receive them. On they came, shrieking at the top of their voices and uttering their war-cries, until they got almost within shot. Seeing this we presented our rifles, but, just at the moment that we were about to fire, the warriors threw themselves over on the opposite side of their horses, and, sweeping by like a whirlwind, discharged their guns.

Although it was a fine exhibition of horsemanship, the fellows, evidently afraid of us, had kept too far off for their object, and the bullets fell short. At the same moment Armitage, Story, and Pierre fired. Armitage's bullet struck the horse of the leading brave, which however still galloped on. Story wounded the next warrior, who turning tail rejoined his companions, while the third—who had lifted up his head to take better aim—got a bullet through it from Pierre's unerring rifle. He fell to the ground, along which he was dragged by his horse, which followed the one immediately before it.

Seeing what had befallen their leaders, the other Indians, who were riding furiously towards us, reined in their steeds, considering discretion the better part of valour.

"We must not trust to the fellows," cried Dick; "we must hold our ground until they move off."

It was fortunate we did so, for in a short time the whole troop, gaining courage and hoping to frighten us with war-whoops, came sweeping down upon us. Fortunately but few had fire-arms, and their powder was none of the best. Their arrows fell short, while their bullets, which struck our saddles, failed to pierce them. I got a slight graze on my cheek, and a piece of lead went through Charley's cap.

Our rifles in the meantime returned the salute in good earnest. Three of us only fired at a time, and three Indians were hit—one of whom was killed outright, 'though his companions managed to drag off his body. Still the odds were greatly against us. Had we been well supplied with ammunition we should have had no fear as to the result of the encounter, but we dared not fire a shot more than was absolutely necessary.

Notwithstanding the way we had handled them, the Indians did not appear inclined to give up the contest, but, after wheeling out of reach of our rifles, again halted.

"They have had enough of it, I should think," observed Story.

"I'm not so sure of that," answered Dick, "our scalps, our horses, and our fire-arms, are too tempting prizes to allow the rascals to let us escape if they fancy that they can get possession of them. See, here they come again!"

As he spoke the whole troop, giving utterance to a terrific war-whoop, passed ahead of us, and then, wheeling round, dashed forward at full speed to attack us on the opposite side. As they got within range, half our number, as before, fired. Three more of them appeared to be hit, and one, evidently a chief, fell from his saddle.

The Redskins had had enough of it, and the rest, crawling round the chief, bore him off. Away they went fleet as the wind. I felt very much inclined to follow. Dick advised us to remain where we were to see what they would do. At length we were satisfied that they had received a lesson by which they were likely to profit, and that they would not again venture to attack us, unless they could take us by surprise. We now found the advantage of not having over-exhausted our horses.

"Mount, and push forward!" cried Dick. "But I say, lads, while those fellows are watching us we'll move at a steady pace."

After we had ridden for a couple of miles or so, Dick advised that we should put our horses to their full speed, so as to place as wide a distance between us and our enemies as possible, before we halted for breakfast.

No sooner was the word given than away we went. Pierre proved an excellent guide, and took us across the most easy country, so that by noon it was considered that we might halt without fear of interruption from the same band, though it would be necessary to keep a sharp look out lest another troop of savages might be scouring the country in search of us.

We were by this time desperately sharp set, and while our steeds cropped the grass around, we quickly lighted our fire and put on our venison to cook. Pierre and the Indians did not wait for that operation, but ate the dried venison raw, and I was tempted to chew the end of a strip to stop the gnawings of hunger.

After a couple of hours' rest, which our horses absolutely required, we again pushed on, anxious to find a safe camping-place for the night. Pierre led us to a spot which appeared as secure as we could desire, by the side of a broad stream of sufficient depth to afford us protection on that side, while a high knoll, with a bluff, would conceal our fire on the one side, and a thick wood on the other, leaving thus only one side towards the prairie. Thus, at all events, we had all the requirements for camping—wood, water, and grass.

The night passed quietly, and the following day we did not fall in with any Indians, so that we ventured to camp at an earlier hour, on a spot very similar to that we had chosen on the previous night. We were getting somewhat tired of our dry venison, and Armitage proposing to go out in search of a deer, I volunteered to accompany him, hoping to find one coming down to drink at the stream. We accordingly kept along its banks, taking with us one of the spare horses, that we might bring home any game we might shoot; but as I wished to give mine a rest I went on foot.

Armitage was some little way in advance, I following close along the borders of the stream, when I heard him fire. Pushing forward I saw him bending over the body of a fine deer. I was making my way through the bushes to assist him, when what was my dismay to catch sight of a huge bear, which Armitage had not perceived, coming along the edge of the stream from the opposite direction.

I shouted to him, to warn him of his danger. He rose to his feet, holding the rein of his horse; for the animal, conscious of the presence of the bear, showed a strong inclination to bolt. The bear, which had, apparently, not before perceived Armitage, came cantering slowly on, until within twenty paces of him. I shouted at the top of my voice for the purpose of distracting the bear's attention; but Bruin, intent on mischief, took no notice. I was too far off to have any hope of mortally wounding the bear should I fire, and the undergrowth was so thick that I could only slowly make my way through it. Already the bear was scarcely more than a dozen paces off from Armitage, who with his gun levelled stood ready to receive his formidable antagonist. The bear raised itself on its hind legs, giving a roaring grunt, and balancing itself, as bears are wont to do, before making its fatal spring. Should Armitage miss, it seemed impossible that he could escape with his life. I struggled desperately to make my way through the brushwood to go to his assistance.

Again the bear roared, and stretched out its paws, evidently showing that it was about to spring, when my friend fired.

Great was my relief when I saw the bear roll over, floundering about for a few seconds in a vain endeavour to rise and renew the combat; but the bullet had been surely aimed, and before I reached the scene of the encounter the animal's struggles were over.

We walked round and round the monster, surveying its vast proportions, and then set to work to remove its hide and cut off the most delicate portions

" AGAIN THE BEAR ROARED, AND STRETCHED OUT ITS PAWS "

of the meat. This occupied us some time. I suggested that the skin might be left behind, but, as the bear was of unusual size, Armitage declared his intention of preserving it if he could. At length we succeeded in strapping it on the back of the horse, and set off to return to the camp.

We walked leisurely along, leading the horse, well satisfied with the result of our short expedition; for bear's flesh, though not equal to venison, is superior to that of the lean deer we often shot. We found our friends anxious about us; for two of the Indians who had gone out scouting reported that they had fallen in with a suspicious trail, and they warned us that we should very likely be again attacked before we could reach the settlement.

"Let them come on then!" cried Dick, "we'll treat them as we did the others."

I have said but little about the Indians accompanying Armitage. They were fine fellows, armed with spears and bows and arrows, as well as with carbines, while they carried in their belts the usual scalping-knives and tomahawks, so that they were likely to prove formidable opponents to our foes.

Having set a double watch, one man to look after the horses, and another the camp, we lay down to obtain the rest we so much needed.

CHAPTER III.

DAYBREAK found us moving forward and already a couple of miles from our last resting-place. We hoped thus to keep ahead of our enemies, who, our Indian allies calculated, had camped some distance to the northward. We thought it probable also, should they have discovered our whereabouts, that they might have intended to attack us before we started in the morning. They would know that we should keep careful watch during the night, but they were very likely to fancy that while breakfasting we should be off our guard, and that they might then take us by surprise. If so, they were disappointed. We rode steadily on, we Whites keeping together, while the Indians on their active mustangs, scouted on either side, their keen eyes searching every thicket and bush for a concealed enemy.

"Can they be trusted?" asked Dick of Armitage.

"They will lose the reward I engaged to give them, should they prove treacherous," was the answer, "and Pierre considers them honest."

"I cannot help suspecting that they are very sure no enemy is near, by the way they are showing off," observed Story.

"They behaved as well as men could do, when we were last attacked," remarked Charley, who was always ready to stick up for the Indians, of whom he had a great admiration. I agreed with Jack, but at the same time I did not wish to disparage our gallant-looking allies.

While we were speaking two of them came up and addressed Pierre in their own language which he understood thoroughly.

" They say that they have caught sight of a mounted war-party, who are, they think, trying to steal upon us round yonder wood, and take us by surprise," said Pierre.

" We'll be prepared for them then, my friends!" exclaimed Dick; " but we'll ride on as we have been going, and not dismount until they show themselves; we shall then be able to turn the tables on them. You all know what you have to do; but remember again, our powder is running short; don't throw a shot away."

" Aye, aye, captain," was the reply from all of us, for we had given Dick a title he well deserved although the Lords of the Admiralty had not thus favoured him.

Our scouts on the left flank now drew in closer to us, they having made up their minds that we should be attacked on that side. Almost ahead—or, as Dick called it, on our starboard bow—was a clump of trees, backed by rocky ground. It would assist at all events to protect us, on one side. We accordingly directed our course towards it. Anyone seeing us riding along would not have supposed that we were

well aware of a powerful body of enemies being close
to us, as we might have been seen laughing and
joking, one of the party occasionally breaking out
into a jovial song.

Our behaviour encouraged our allies, and should
the enemy have perceived us, it would have made
them suppose that we were quite unconscious of their
presence.

We had almost gained the clump of trees I have
mentioned, when from the end of the wood about half
a mile away, appeared the head of a column of
mounted warriors. The moment they showed themselves, with fierce yells and shrieks they dashed on
towards us. "Forward, my friends, and let us take
up the post I proposed," cried Dick; and, urging our
horses into a gallop, we reached the clump just in
time to dismount and arrange our horses before the
Indians got within range of our rifles. We were
thus better able to defend ourselves than we had
been on the previous occasion. The Coomanches
came on bravely enough at first, shrieking and hoot-
ing at the top of their voices, but we were prepared
to receive them in a way they did not expect. Before
they began to wheel and throw themselves over on
the sides of their horses, Armitage, Story and I, who
were considered the best shots of the party, each
singled out a man. We fired, and three warriors
dropped to the ground. At the same moment, our
brave allies dashed forward, with lances in rest, and
charged boldly at the advancing foe, who were discharging a shower of arrows at us. One of the
Coomanches threw himself on the side of his horse

and shot an arrow which pierced our friend's shoulder, but he was himself the next instant thrust through by his opponent's lance, his horse galloping off, however, with his dead body. This bold manœuvre gave us time to reload. We were able to fire a volley as the rest of the party came sweeping by. Two more saddles were emptied, and another warrior was wounded. The latter, however, managed to regain his seat so as to wheel round and rejoin his companions.

Had we been a more numerous party, and armed with swords and lances, we might have mounted and pursued the enemy; but as we possessed only our rifles, it was far more prudent to remain on foot, whence we could take a steady aim.

It was surprising to see the way our persevering assailants came on, and threw themselves over the sides of their horses. It was not until we had an opportunity of examining their trappings, that we discovered how they managed to do so. We found attached to the mane of each horse a strong halter composed of horse-hair, which being passed under the animal's neck, was firmly plaited into the mane, thus leaving a loop hanging under its neck. When about to fire, the warrior drops into this loop, and he manages to sustain the weight of his body by the upper part of the bent arm. In this way, both his arms are at liberty, either to use his bow or his spear. In his left hand he grasps a dozen arrows, together with his bow, and is not compelled to apply his hand to his quiver, which hangs with his shield at his back, while his long spear being

E

supported by the bend of the elbow he can use it at any moment.

Our allies, on this occasion, rendered us essential service by distracting the attention of our active foes, thus preventing them from shooting with as much accuracy as usual. Their arrows came flying about us, many sticking in the trees behind our backs; but happily only two of our people and one of our horses were slightly wounded, although one of our Indian allies fell to the ground, and before any of his companions could rescue him, a Coomanche, who had ridden up, leaning over his horse, took his scalp and rejoined the main body.

The steady fire we kept up, prevented the Indians from coming close to us; still they were evidently unwilling to abandon the attempt, in spite of the numbers they had already lost. As far as we could judge, the party which had before attacked us had been increased by many fresh warriors, eager to distinguish themselves. Could they obtain the white men's scalps, they would be able to boast of their achievement to the end of their days.

We had no intention, could we help it, of giving them this satisfaction. One thing was remarkable — the regular way in which they came on and retreated, like any civilized people engaging in warfare. Our allies, after our first attack, had rejoined us, and waited close at hand to dash forward again, should they see a favourable opportunity. At length the Coomanches, having swept round out of rifle-shot, disappeared behind the wood from which they had emerged. No sooner had they gone, than our allies threw themselves

INDIAN HORSEMEN IN CONFLICT.

from their horses and dashed forward towards the bodies of the slain. In vain Dick shouted to Pierre to tell them to let the carcases alone. Never did I witness a more horrid sight; with their scalp-knives in their hands, they sprang forward, and in an instant had passed the sharp blades round the heads of two of them. A third, though badly wounded, both by one of our bullets and an arrow in his side, raised himself up, and fiercely regarding his advancing foe, mocked and derided him as an ally of the whites.

The Indian advanced, and springing on the prostrate man, without waiting to give him the merciful blow, whipped off his scalp, and left him still bleeding on the ground. On seeing this, Pierre, who seemed rather ashamed of his friends, sent a bullet into the poor wretch's head, and put him out of his misery.

The knife of one of the others must have been blunt, for finding that the scalp did not come off as quickly as he wished, seating himself on the ground with his feet against the dead man's shoulders, he pulled it away by main force. So far we had been more successful than we had expected; but our enemies might rally, and, hovering in the neighbourhood, keep us constantly in a state of anxiety. We were unwilling to leave our secure position until we could ascertain whether the Indians had retreated. To learn this, it was necessary to get to the other side of the wood, which hid them from view. For this purpose, one of our allies volunteered to ride forward and ascertain where they were. The risk, however, was great, for should he be pursued, and overtaken, his death was certain. Still, the advantage to us

INDIANS SCALPING THE SLAIN AND WOUNDED.

would be so great, that Armitage consented to his going. Instead of making directly towards the wood, however, he rode first to the east and then suddenly turning his course northward, galloped along at full speed, until he got a good view of the north side of the wood which was a mere belt of trees, scarcely thick enough to conceal a large body of horsemen.

We watched him anxiously. At any moment his enemies might sally out and attack him. At length we saw him turn his horse's head, when he came riding leisurely back. Perceiving this we forthwith mounted and continued our journey, leaving the bodies of the Indians to be devoured by the prairie wolves, for we had no time, even had we wished it, to bury them.

We of course kept a bright look out behind us as well as on either side, for as Pierre observed, "It never does to trust those varmints of Redskins; they come like the wind, and are off again with as many scalps as they can lift before a man who has shut his eyes for a moment has time to open them."

I confess that I heartily hoped we should in future be left alone; for, although I had no objection to an occasional brush with the red men, I had no fancy to be constantly harassed by them, and to be compelled to remain in camp without the chance of a shot at a deer or buffalo for fear of losing one's scalp. I thought, however, that we had now done with them and should the next night be able to sleep in peace. Again we continued on until it was nearly dark, when we formed camp in as sheltered ·a position as we could find.

Of course our trail would show the way we had taken, and, should the Indians be so disposed, they might follow us. The only question was whether they could or could not take us by surprise. We had, fortunately, enough meat for supper, but we agreed that it would be necessary to hunt the next day at all risks. When, however, we came to examine our powder horns, we found that we had scarcely more than a couple of charges each. It would be impossible therefore to defend ourselves, should we be again attacked, and a difficult task to obtain game sufficient to last us to the end of the journey. We had fortunately a good supply of bear's meat, which, as Dick observed, " went a long way ; " but our Indian friends were voracious feeders and it was necessary to give them as much as they wanted. Our chief hope now of obtaining food was that we might come across some buffalo which our Indians would be able to shoot with their bows and arrows : at all events, having already escaped so many dangers, we determined to keep up our spirits and not to be cast down by the difficulties in the way.

As our Indians had been on the watch the previous night, we undertook to keep guard this night, two at a time. Charley and I were to be together.

What the captain called " the middle watch " was over, when we mounted guard, Charley on the horses, I on the camp. Just then the moon, in its last quarter, rose above the horizon, shedding a pale light over the prairie. We had been on foot a couple of hours and I was hoping that it would soon be time to

rouse up my companions and commence the day's
march, when Charley came to me.

" Look there!" he said, " I fancy that I can make
out some objects in the distance, but whether they
are prairie wolves or men I am not quite certain. If
they are Indians, the sooner we secure the horses the
better. If they are wolves they can do us no great
harm. We will awaken our friends, at all events!"

I quickly, in a low voice, called up all hands;
and each man, without standing on his feet, crept
towards his horse. In a few seconds we had secured
the whole of them.

"Now!" cried Dick, "mount and away."

No sooner were the words uttered, than we sprang
into our saddles. As we did so a loud shout saluted
our ears, followed by the whistling of arrows; and,
turning round, we saw fifty dark forms scampering
after us. Had we possessed ammunition, we should
not have dreamed of taking to flight; but, without
the means of defending ourselves, it was the only safe
thing to be done. The arrows came fast and thick.

" Keep together lads," cried Dick, " never mind
those bodkins, we shall soon distance our pursuers."

I heard a sharp cry from Charley and turning round
I saw an arrow sticking in his side. The captain had
already been wounded, but he did not betray the fact
of his being hurt.

Our horses, seeming to understand our dangerous
position, stretched out at their greatest speed. I
turned round and could still see the Indians coming
on and discharging their arrows; but we were now
beyond their range, and, provided our horses kept

their feet, we had no fear of being overtaken. It was very trying to have to run away from foes whom we had twice defeated, for we had no doubt that they were the same band of Redskins we had before en-countered and who now hoped, by approaching on foot, to take us by surprise. Had not Charley's quick sight detected them indeed, we should probably have lost our horses and have been murdered into the bargain. On we galloped, yet for a long time we could hear the shrieks and shouts of our distant foes. Their horses were not likely to be far off, and we knew that they would probably return for them and again pursue us. We must, therefore, put a considerable distance between ourselves and them. Fortunately, not having tired our steeds, we should be able to go on without pulling rein for the whole day; we must, however, camp to feed them, but not for a moment longer than would be absolutely necessary for the purpose. I asked Charley how he felt.

"Never mind me," he answered, "the arrow hurts somewhat, but I would not have our party stop to attend to me. If I feel worse I'll tell you, lest I should drop from my horse."

The captain said not a word of his wound, nor did anyone else complain of being hurt; though, as day-light increased, I observed blood streaming from the leg of one of the Indians, and another with a pierced coat through which an arrow had gone. At length our steeds gave signs of being tired, and we ourselves had become very hungry. We agreed, therefore, to pull up near a stream, with a knoll close to it, from which we could obtain, through our spy-glasses, a wide view across the prairie, so that we could see our enemies before they could discover us. To light a fire and cook our bear's flesh while our horses were turned loose to feed, occupied but little time. We had saved a couple of tin mugs with which we brought water from the stream; but our kettle, and several other articles, in the hurry of our flight, had been left behind. Our first care was to see to Charley's wound. He heroically bore the operation of cutting off the head of the arrow, which had to be done before the shaft of the arrow could be drawn out. We then, with a handkerchief, bound up the wound. Dick was less seriously hurt, an arrow having, however, torn its way through his shoulder. The Indian made light of his wound which was very similar to that Charley had received. His companions doctored him, we supplying them with a handkerchief which they bound round his wounded limb. I was still resting when Story, who had taken his post on the knoll, spy-glass in hand, shouted out—

"I have just caught sight of the heads of the Redskins, over the grass, so the sooner we are away the better."

Saying this he hurried down the hill. We, having caught the horses and packed up the remainder of our meat, mounted and rode on. Both Charley and Dick declared they did not feel much the worse for their wounds, the blood they had lost probably preventing inflammation. Though the Indians could not see us, they must have discovered our trail; and they would soon ascertain, by the remains of our fire, that we were not far ahead. This might encourage them to pursue us; but our horses being better than theirs, we might still, should no accident happen, keep well ahead of them.

We galloped on until dark and then we were once more compelled to camp. Only half our party lay down at a time, the remainder keeping by the horses while they fed, to be ready to bring them in at a moment's notice. Our pursuers would also have to stop to feed their horses, and as they had not come up to us during the first watch, we hoped that they would leave us in quiet for the remainder of the night.

We were not disturbed; and before daybreak, jumping into our saddles, we pushed on. I must pass over the two following days. As yet we had met with no signs of civilization, when we saw a wreath of smoke rising above the trees in the far distance. It might come from a backwoodsman's hut, or it might be simply that of a camp fire. It was not likely to rise from the camp of Indians, so Pierre thought, as they do not generally venture so far east. However, to run no risk of falling among foes, we sent forward one of our scouts, while we proceeded at the pace we had before been going. We felt most anxious to get some shelter, where we could sleep in security and obtain food, for our bear's flesh was well-nigh exhausted, and we had not hitherto fallen in with buffalo; while both our wounded men required more care than we could give them in the camp, with the chance of having to mount and ride for our lives at any moment.

After riding some distance we heard a shot.

"All's not right," cried Dick; "we may have either to fight, or run for it."

In a short time we saw an Indian riding at full speed towards us.

"What's the matter?" asked Pierre as he came near.

He pointed to the wood, when presently two white men appeared with rifles in their hands. As soon as they caught sight of us, they shouted out and made signs of friendship to us, while they grounded their arms. We were soon up to them.

"Sorry to have shot at your Redskin friend, but we took him for an enemy, that's a fact," said one of them; "however, as the bit of lead missed his head, he's none the worse for it."

Dick assured him we had no wish to complain, and asked whether we could find any shelter in the neighbourhood.

"You are welcome to our hut, friends," answered the other man, "it's big enough for all hands except the Indians, and they can put up wigwams for themselves. Come along, for there's a storm brewing, I guess; and you'll be better under cover than in the open air."

We gladly accepted the invitation, and guided by our new acquaintances, we soon found ourselves in a clearing, with a good-sized log-hut and a couple of shanties at the rear of it. The rain had already begun to fall; so speedily taking off the bridles and saddles of our steeds, we hobbled them and turned them loose; we then hurried under cover, our Indian guides taking possession of one of the shanties.

Our hosts, Mark and Simon Praeger, told us that

they and their brothers had built the log-hut the previous winter. They had already a good-sized field fenced in and under cultivation and had besides a herd of cattle, the intention of the family being to move west in a few months.

On hearing of the loss of our provisions and stores, they at once set to work to get supper ready; and, as they had killed a deer that morning and had a good supply of flour, coffee and other articles, they soon placed an abundant meal smoking on the table. We at once discovered that they were superior to the general run of backwoodsmen, having a fair education, at the same time that they were hardy persevering fellows, and bold buffalo and deer hunters, who held the Redskins in supreme contempt. Their family, they told us, resided somewhere about a hundred miles away to the eastward. They had pushed thus far into the wilderness to form a home for themselves, both young men intending to marry shortly and set up house. Their father's farm was close to the very settlement for which we were bound, and the nearest where we were likely to get our wants amply supplied. They were sure, they said, that their father would be happy to receive us and assist us in obtaining all we required. We thanked them and gladly accepted their kind offer.

Supper being over, we lay down in our buffalo robes; and I need scarcely say that, having no longer the fear of being aroused by finding an Indian's scalp-ing-knife running round my head, I was quickly fast asleep, fully expecting to have a good night's rest.

My sleep, however, at length became troubled. I

dreamed that I heard the Indian war-whoops, and saw a whole band of savages spring out of the darkness and rush with uplifted tomahawks towards me while I lay helpless on the ground. Presently the cries increased, and I awoke with a start to hear a terrific growling sound. It was that of a bear, I was convinced. I saw that Mark Praeger, having got up and struck a light, had taken down his rifle from the wall and was going towards the door. I jumped up, as did Armitage and Story, and followed him. As he threw open the door, we saw, not a dozen paces from the hut, a huge bear squatting on his hindquarters and apparently taking a leisurely survey of the hut.

Mark, as soon as he caught sight of his visitor, lifted his rifle and fired, but the cap failed to go off. It would have been a fine opportunity for Bruin to have made a rush upon us; when he might, by dashing into the hut, have taken possession and killed us all one after the other, or driven us out. Instead of doing so, alarmed by the shouts we raised, uttering a low growl, he turned round and broke away through the brushwood on one side of the hut.

"On lads!" cried Mark, "we must get that fellow for the sake of the meat and skin."

As he spoke he replaced the copper cap and dashed forward in pursuit of the intruder. As we had no wish to go bear-hunting unarmed, we hurried back to obtain our rifles and some powder and bullets from Simon. By the time we were supplied, the rest of the party who had been aroused by our shouts, were on foot and preparing to accompany us. On returning to the

MARK PRAEGER AND THE BEAR.

door, we could nowhere see Mark; but Simon taking the lead we followed him. The moon had got up, so that we managed to see our way with tolerable clearness, by a path leading down to a stream, with precipitous banks, rising in some places into cliffs of considerable height. We had gone some distance when we heard a shot fired.

"Mark has brought Master Bruin to bay," cried Simon; "I wish he had waited until we had come up."

I heard the sound of footsteps behind us, and looking round saw that our Indian allies had followed, as eager as we were to get the bear's meat. Just then we saw Mark bending over the bear which he had shot; but what was our horror the next moment to observe another huge monster rush out from behind a rock and lifting itself on its haunches make a spring at him, before he could even turn round to defend himself. His death seemed certain. In attempting to shoot the bear, we should too probably kill him. No one therefore dared to fire. In vain he endeavoured to escape from the claws of the creature who held him in a fast embrace. His brother and Armitage, who were leading, dashed forward, the one drawing a long knife, the other armed with an axe which he had caught up as we left the hut. I held my gun ready, waiting to fire should I be able to do so without running the risk of shooting one of my friends.

It was a fearful moment. It seemed scarcely possible, even should we kill the bear, that poor Mark would escape destruction. Simon, springing close to the monster, dealt it a tremendous blow with his axe,

A "FEARFUL MOMENT" FOR MARK PRAEGER

1

hoping to draw its attention on himself; while Armitage, with his uplifted knife, dashed forward, and as he did so plunged his weapon behind the bear's shoulder. The monster turned round on feeling the wound, and I thought would have bitten Mark's head. Simon again plied the brute with his axe. The huge jaws relaxed, the head sank down, Armitage had driven his knife home to the beast's heart.

With shouts, indicative of their satisfaction, the Indians now hurried up and assisted us in dragging off the body from our fallen friend who was by this time nearly senseless. The bear's claws had torn him fearfully about the breast and shoulders, besides having given him a tremendous hug, but had, we hoped, injured no vital part. He was unable, however, to speak or stand. We at once, therefore, formed a litter with poles speedily cut from the banks of the stream, on which we bore him back to the hut, leaving the Indians under the command of Pierre to cut up the bears and bring in their flesh and skins, an occupation to which they applied themselves with evident delight.

CHAPTER IV.

ON arriving at the hut with our almost inanimate burden, we found the captain and Charlie in a state of great anxiety to know what had happened; for they had, I should have said, been undressed, and placed in our hosts' beds, their wounds preventing them from putting on their clothes. The captain insisted on turning out when he saw the sad condition of Mark; and he moreover undertook to doctor him as well as he was able. It appeared evident, however, that as soon as possible Mark and Charley should be removed to the settlement, where they could obtain surgical aid. Mark in a short time revived. From the captain's report, we had hopes that, on account of his fine constitution, he would escape inflammation, which was chiefly, under his circumstances, to be feared.

The Praegers had a light wagon, into which, soon after breakfast was over the next morning, we put our three wounded companions, and leaving Pierre and the Indians with Simon Praeger, we set off for Tillydrone. We would gladly have had another day's rest, but the impossibility of obtaining medical assistance for poor Mark and Charley made us willing to undergo the fatigue.

The country was tolerably level, there being a fine open prairie, across which we rattled at a good speed, though the unavoidable jolting must have greatly tried our poor friends within. I was very thankful when Mark, looking out of the wagon, told us that we were approaching his father's house. Our cavalcade must have been seen, for in a short time two horsemen came galloping up to us: the elder, a fine-looking, middle-aged man, Mark saluted as his father; the other as brother Peter. A few words explained what had happened. Mr. Praeger immediately invited us all to his house, while Peter started off as fast as he could go to summon the doctor.

The house to which we were conducted was a picturesque, comfortable-looking building, constructed of wood, with a low pitched roof, and wide long verandah, up to which a flight of broad steps led us. We found a matronly-looking dame, with a bevy of young ones, standing in the verandah, evidently wondering at the number of guests Mr. Praeger was bringing to the house. They were all activity on hearing the state of the occupants of the wagon, and hurried down the steps to assist in lifting in our wounded companions, for neither Charley nor Mark were able to walk. The captain, however, got up the steps by merely leaning on Mr. Praeger's arm.

In a few minutes all three were placed in bed, Mrs. Praeger declaring that it was the only place fit for either of them, though her son was certainly the most hurt.

The young ladies were so busy during the evening, flitting about here and there, that I could scarcely tell how many there were of them. I remarked, however, that one was taller than the others, very fair, and with a graceful figure. When Armitage—who had remained out of sight, looking after the horses—came in, she was not in the room, and it was some time before she returned. When she did so, he rose to his feet, and regarded her earnestly, while the colour mounted to his cheek and brow; then he bowed, and stood apparently irresolute whether to advance or retreat. She started on seeing him and then put out her hand. He sprang across the room and took it.

" I little expected to have the happiness of seeing you, Miss Hargrave," he said.

" Is it a happiness?" she asked, in a calm tone.

" Indeed it is," he replied. " I heard that you had left England, but could not ascertain to what part of the world you had gone."

What further passed between our friend and the young lady I cannot tell, as they lowered their voices, while they retired to a window at the other end of the room, Armitage forgetting all about his supper.

The ladies of the family, I should say, did not sit down to table, as they had already taken their evening meal, and insisted on waiting upon us.

Peter Praeger returned sooner than was expected with the doctor, whom he found on a visit to a family five or six miles off.

He gave a more favourable report of Dick and Charley than I expected, but young Mark, he said, would require the greatest possible care ; a good constitution, however, he hoped, would enable him to pull through, though his hurts were of a most serious description.

I had no opportunity of speaking to Armitage before turning in, so I was unable to ascertain more about the young lady he had so unexpectedly met. The rest of the family were very nice and pretty girls, their manners much superior to what I had reasonably supposed would be found in the " Far West."

Soon after breakfast the next morning, I saw Armitage and Miss Hargrave walking out together, he having asked her to show him a beautiful view she had spoken of at the other end of the estate. The rest of the young ladies being occupied, Story and I lit our pipes, and were sitting smoking them in the verandah, when we were joined by Mr. Praeger.

" Your companion appears to be an old friend of my young relative," he observed, as if apparently wishing to learn something about Armitage.

I replied that he was well known to Lieutenant Buntin, who spoke highly of him ; and that he was evidently a man of some means, as we judged from his outfit and the number of his attendants, while we had found him a most excellent fellow in every respect.

" I'm glad to hear it, for the sake of my wife's young cousin Ellen," he answered. " She came out to us a few months ago, having lost her parents, and having no relatives for whom she cared in England. She had, however, very little idea of the rough style of life we are compelled to lead ; but she at once got into our ways, though I observed what I could not account for, that she was often more melancholy than was consistent with her disposition. Now, however, I suspect the cause."

I fully agreed with our out-spoken host. I soon found that we were not likely to learn anything of the interesting subject from Armitage himself, for he was remarkably reticent, and I saw that it would not do to banter him, or allude in any way to it.

I must pass over several days, during which the doctor as well as the ladies of the family were unremitting in their attentions to the wounded men. The captain was soon himself again, though still too weak to travel; but Charley's wound took much longer to heal, and Mark was not likely to be on foot again for three or four weeks at soonest. In the meantime, Story and I, with our constant companion, Peter, rode over to the settlement to obtain the stores we required for our journey, as well as to replace our baggage mules.

While thus engaged, we found an old trapper also making purchases at the stores. He was tall and gaunt, his countenance weather beaten and sunburnt, of a ruddy brown hue, his hair—which hung over his shoulders—being only slightly grizzled, while his chin and face were smooth shaved. He was dressed in a hunting-frock of buckskin, and pantaloons of the same material ornamented down the seams with long fringes. On his feet he wore mocassins of Indian make; his head was covered by a neatly-made cap of beaver; an unusually large powder-horn was slung over his shoulders, together with a rifle, carefully covered up; while in his belt, in addition to a knife and tomakawk, he carried a brace of pistols with long barrels, showing that he was accustomed to travel amongst enemies, and was prepared to make a stout fight if he was attacked. On seeing us, he enquired who we were, where we had come from, and in what direction we were going.

We told him without hesitation.

"I guess the old hoss will go with you some of the way," he said. "Tell Master Praeger that Ben Folkard will pay him a visit before long, I can't say when. He knows me, and he knows when I say I'll do a thing I intend to do it."

We promised to give old Folkard's message, and soon afterwards we parted from him. Peter told us that he had heard his father speak of Ben Folkard as one of the most noted and skilful trappers of the Rocky Mountains, and that he never turned up without a large supply of skins and peltries.

We were fortunate in obtaining some fine Mexican mules and all the articles we required, though we had to pay somewhat highly for them. Well satisfied, we set off to return to Mr. Praeger's. The houses and the stores were few and far between, the intermediate country being still in a state of nature. As our laden mules could not travel fast, we had to camp on the way. We chose a grassy spot near a wood, offering sufficient attractions to our animals to prevent them from straying, though of course we hobbled them as an additional security.

While Peter remained in camp, Story and I took our guns to get a turkey, or any other game which might come in our way. We had not gone far when

Story called my attention to an animal standing on
the fallen trunk of a tree, and told me to keep back
the dogs, which would be sure to suffer if they were to
attack it. I was about to fire, when I caught sight of
another animal of similar size with a long, thin body
and sharp nose, which I at once recognised as a
marten. It had apparently been watching the porcupine, who, unconscious of its approach, remained
perfectly still, its spines scarcely visible. The marten
was intent on taking its enemy by surprise; and,
stealing up, threw itself on the unsuspicious porcupine before it had time even to raise its spines. The
moment it felt itself seized, it began to lash its tail
about and throw out its quills in all directions; but
the marten, by its wonderful agility, escaped the
blows aimed at it. In a short time it gained the
victory, and was already sucking the blood of its
victim when Story fired and hit it in the head. As
the skin was of considerable value, we quickly flayed
it, and with a couple of turkeys which we were fortunate enough to shoot, returned to camp, where, to
our surprise, we found old Folkard seated smoking
his pipe.

"I'm going along with you, boys," he said. "Good
company isn't always to be got, and it's not always
safe, while the Redskins are on the war-path, to
travel through the country alone. You can help me
and I can help you, so that we shall be quits."

We, of course, told the trapper that we should be
very happy to have the benefit of his experience.

We passed the night quietly enough; but the next
morning, to our excessive disgust, half the mules

A MARTEN KILLING A PORCUPINE.

were missing. In spite of their hobbles, they had
managed to get away. Peter and I with two men at
once set off in search of them ; but it was not until
late in the day that we found the runaways. As soon
as we had brought them back we started, but of
course could make but a short distance. On camping,
with the assistance of the old trapper we hobbled
them more securely than on the previous night, and
by his advice a watch was set, we all taking the duty
in turns. Old Ben, however, excused himself from
watching, declaring that his mules never ran away
and that as he should have to keep wide awake during
most nights by and by, he should prefer a sound sleep
while he could get it.

To this we made no objection. We placed the
packs on one side of our camp-fire, near which, having
taken our suppers, the old trapper, Peter, and Story
lay down to sleep; while I, with my rifle in my hand,
walked off to look after the horses and mules. I kept
walking up and down, keeping my eyes open, and
when any of the animals appeared inclined to head
off from the rest turned them back. The night was
fine and the stars shone out brightly, but it was otherwise somewhat dark. At last I began to yawn and
to wish heartily that Story would come and relieve
me. Once or twice I heard cries in the distance very
similar to those which had disturbed us when further
to the west, but here, so near the settled districts, I
thought nothing of the matter. I suspected that the
cunning mules were watching me, for when I turned
towards the camp to call Story, off one or two of
them bolted. They had played me this trick two or

WOLVES MAKING OFF WITH OUR BAGGAGE. *p. 78.*

three times, and at last one of them led me so long a chase that when I caught him I determined to punish the brute by securing him to a tree. Having done so I turned towards the camp, but the fire had burnt so low that I could scarcely see the spot. There was light enough, however, to enable me to distinguish several objects moving over the ground. Can they be Indians? I thought, as I ran forward hoping to arouse my companions in time to defend themselves. Before I got up to the camp, however, I saw what I at once knew to be a pack of wolves. On they came without bark or yelp, making straight for our baggage. Among the provisions we had purchased was a quantity of pemmican placed on the top. I really believe that the wolves, cunning as foxes, had surveyed our camp and knew exactly what to go in for. I shouted loudly, hoping to frighten them off and awaken my friends; but even old Ben was sleeping so soundly that for some time no one heard my voice, while I was afraid to fire at the wolves for fear—in the uncertain light—of hitting one of my sleeping companions.

At length up sprang Story and Peter, and their cries aroused the old trapper. It was too late, however, to prevent the wolves making an onslaught on our baggage. Each seized something in his mouth, but our cries prevented them from remaining and devouring the whole of our provisions, which they undoubtedly otherwise would have done. Off they went, several of the rascals carrying bags of pemmican or of flour, or packages of hams in their mouths. I fired and stopped the career of one of them, while my companions, imitating my example, shot three others. We then, having reloaded, made chase and brought down two or three more.

We should have regained the whole of our pro- visions, but, in several instances, the moment a wolf was shot another brute seized his prize and made off with it. Under other circumstances we should not have expended powder on the brutes. We fired away, however, as long as any remained within shot, and on searching for the booty we recovered nearly the whole of it. Our chief loss was in our flour, as the animals, while grabbing the bags from each other, had well nigh torn them to pieces and let the contents run out.

Old Ben took matters very coolly, but Story and Peter were so vexed that they undertook to ride back and replace our loss, if we would consent to move on slowly with the rest of the animals. This we gladly did, the old trapper managing them with perfect ease. He said that he had seldom known a pack of wolves to come so far east, and advised that in future we should keep a sharp look-out lest we might encounter others.

Our friends overtook us the next day, and in the evening we reached Mr. Praeger's. We found Dick quite recovered and ready to set off again; but it seemed doubtful whether Armitage would continue his expedition. It struck me that although Mr. Praeger was very civil, he would be glad to have us go. To say the least, we occupied a great deal of the attention of the ladies of the family, and Charley hinted that honest Dick was somewhat spoony on one of them. Story had also been warm in his praises of another, and it struck me that the young lady's colour heightened and her eyes brightened when he spoke to her.

Mr. Praeger seemed less contented with his location than I should have thought. He had evidently been captivated by the accounts of the wealth of California, and he made his "woman kind" somewhat uneasy by talking of travelling across the country, bag and baggage, to settle in the new Eldorado. They evidently had no wish to move; which was but natural, as they appeared to me to have everything they could desire, besides being free from the risk of Indian raids to which the settlers farther west were constantly exposed. Dick, Story and I now made active preparations for our departure; and, to my surprise, and much to our satisfaction, Armitage expressed his intention of accompanying us.

I thought that Ellen's countenance and those of some of the other young ladies had a shade of sadness on them as they saw us engaged in doing up our packs and trying our newly-bought mules. Dick and I each purchased a strong, active horse from Mr. Praeger, for which we gave him long prices as some return for his hospitality; and we then presented him with our own steeds, which were likely to pick up muscle and flesh on his rich pastures.

Though he was as courteous as ever, he did not press us to stay, and at length, all our traps being prepared, we set off, accompanied by old Folkard, who did not even ask whether we wished for his society or not. Armitage remained behind, so I did not witness his parting with Miss Hargrave, but he

soon galloped after us. Peter accompanied us as far
as his brother's, to take the place of poor Mark, who
was still unfit for work, though in a fair way of recovery. We spent a day with the young backwoodsmen, whose hearts were delighted with a present of a
first-rate Joe Manton. Our intention was to push on
for the base of the Rocky Mountains to a region
where deer and buffalo and big-horns abounded. We
shot several deer, but as we had come across no
buffalo, the larger herds had, we supposed, moved
northward. We had encamped one afternoon earlier
than usual, being tempted to halt by a wide stream
and a wood near at hand. Our fire being lighted and
our meat put on to roast and stew, Armitage, Story,
and I took our guns to go out in search of turkeys or
other small game, should we be unable to find deer.
Armitage took two of his dogs, though they often
gave us more trouble than assistance in hunting. We
had, however, been tolerably successful, and shot
three fine gobblers and some smaller birds, when,
as we were returning towards camp, the dogs gave
tongue and started off to the right, refusing to return
at their master's call.

We hurried on as fast as the rough nature of the
ground would allow us. We were on the top of some
low cliffs which had formed at some time or other of
the world's history the side of a torrent now dried
up and overgrown with trees. Presently we heard a
cry of—

" Here, boys, help, help ! "

At the same time one of the dogs leaped over the
cliff, and we saw a short distance from us Charley

G

struggling with a brown bear, providentially not a grizzly, which with great courage he had grasped by the throat so as to prevent the brute from biting him; but he was brought on his knees, his cap had fallen off, and his gun lay on the ground beside him. In another instant the bear would have seized his head, when the dog leaped down on the creature's back and caused a diversion in his favour. To fire would have been dangerous, for had we tried to kill the bear we should have run a fearful risk of shooting Charley. We therefore trusted to the assistance of the dogs, the other, following its companion, having fixed its teeth well into the bear. Charley manfully continued the contest, but was afraid of releasing his hold of the bear's throat lest it should bite him.

We shouted and shrieked, hoping to frighten Bruin, as we scrambled over the rocks. At length Charley, still holding the bear's throat with one hand, managed to get hold of his knife with the other, and in spite of the creature's claws round his waist, using all his strength he struck the weapon into its breast. The bear opened its paws as it felt the knife entering, and Charley, having driven the weapon home, sprang back, when the creature rolled over, almost crushing one of the dogs in its convulsive struggles. Before we could get up to the scene of the contest it was dead, and most thankful were we to find Charley wonderfully little injured, though his clothes were somewhat torn. Our young friend showed indeed remarkable nerve, for he scarcely even trembled, though his cheek was somewhat paler than usual from the desperate exertions he had made.

"HE STRUCK THE WEAPON INTO ITS BREAST"

On examining the bear we found that it was an old one, and somewhat thin from want of food; its claws also were blunted from old age, which circumstance accounted for Charley's almost miraculous escape, for had it possessed its full strength a single hug would have pressed the life out of his body.

We congratulated him heartily on his preserva tion, and complimented him on the courage he had exhibited.

"Let us have the skin, at all events," he said. "I would sooner carry it on my own shoulders into camp than leave it behind."

"We'll not disappoint you, my boy," said Story; and he immediately began to flay the animal; but as its flesh was likely to prove tough, we left the carcase for the benefit of the prairie wolves.

While Story and I carried the skin between us, Armitage assisted Charley, who was less able to walk than he had at first supposed. A man cannot get even a moderate hug from a bear without suffering.

At the camp we found two strange Indians, who seemed disposed to be very friendly, and invited us to pay them a visit at their lodges only an hour's march off. One of them was a fine young fellow, dressed in a leathern jacket and leggings richly orna- mented, while on his head he wore a circlet of feathers. He appeared to be greatly struck with Charley on hearing of his exploit with the bear, and putting out his hand, declared that they must henceforth be ' brothers.

Dick, though greatly delighted at hearing of Charley's behaviour, was much concerned on seeing the injuries he had received, which were more serious than we had at first supposed. He insisted on his turning into a hut which old Folkard and Pierre immediately set to work to construct.

Our guests begged that he might be conveyed to their wigwams, saying that their squaws would doctor him and soon restore his strength.

" They may be honest—those Shianees—but they may be rogues like many other Redskins," observed old Ben. " Better not trust them."

We therefore thanked our guests, but declined their offer for the present, saying that our young companion was unfit to be moved, though we hoped to pay them a visit on the following day.

They, nothing abashed, continued to squat round the fire, smoking tobacco and quaffing with evident pleasure the small glasses of usquebaugh which Dick bestowed upon them. Armitage objected, however, to the captain's giving them liquor.

" Let them take as much as they've a fancy to," said Ben. " It wont do them any harm once in a way, and it will let us know what they are thinking about."

Our guests having drunk the whisky, showed the same friendly disposition as at first, nor did they complain when Dick refused to give them any more.

" A little do good, too much do harm," observed Dick, at which they nodded as if perfectly agreeing with him.

As the shades of evening approached, they got up, and shaking hands all round, took their departure.

" They're all right, we may trust them," said Ben.

We nevertheless kept a strict watch over our cattle, for the temptation to steal a fine stud might have been too great for our Indian neighbours to resist. No attempt was made on the camp however, and the next morning the animals were found feeding as quietly as usual.

CHAPTER V.

A TREMENDOUS storm, such as we had not yet experienced, kept us in camp the next morning. The lightning flashed, the thunder roared, and the rain came down in torrents, compelling us to make trenches round our huts. Even when doing this, we were nearly wet to the skin. Our fires also were almost extinguished, though we contrived to keep them in by heaping up fresh fuel every few minutes. It was truly a battle between the flames and the rain, but the former would have been beaten without our assistance. The same cause probably kept the Indians inside their wigwams, for we saw nothing of them. We managed to cover up poor Charley so that he did not suffer. In the afternoon, the rain cleared off, and trusting to the professions of the Indians, Dick and I set off to pay them a visit. For prudence, according to the custom we had adopted, we wore our swords by our sides, at which, as they appeared rather more for ornament than use, the Indians were not likely to take offence. One of the Indians, who had come to our camp the previous evening, was, we discovered, their chief, by name Ocuno, or the Yellow Wolf. He received us with outstretched hands, appearing highly pleased at our coming, and without hesitation introduced us to his principal squaw, a very attractive young woman with a pleasing expression of countenance, and much fairer than Indians in general, indeed we had no doubt that she must have had a white father. She told us that she was much attached to the whites, and had not it been her lot to become the wife of Yellow Wolf, she would gladly have married a pale face. Dick was so well satisfied, that he agreed to bring his young friend over to their village the next morning, that he might be placed under her charge.

The Yellow Wolf told us that he intended to start in search of buffalo in a day or two, and that if we chose, we might accompany him, promising that we should have half the animals slain; "for," as he observed, "he and his people were more expert hunters, yet our firearms would make amends for our want of skill."

After spending some time with our new friends, we returned to our own camp. The offer of Yellow Wolf was accepted by all hands, and in the morning we conveyed Charley on a litter to his lodge, the baggage mules and spare horses being also moved forward to the neighbourhood of the village. We found the Indians preparing to engage in a dance, which we supposed was for our entertainment, but which we afterwards discovered, was for the sake of inducing the Good Spirit to send herds of buffalo to their neighbourhood.

As soon as Charley was comfortably placed inside his wigwam, and the fair Manoa, the "Flower of the

Prairies "—as her lord was wont to call her—was examining his hurts, the Yellow Wolf desired us to be seated in front of it. Scarcely had we taken our places, than from every hut rushed forward some monstrous figures with buffalo heads, but the legs of men and huge tails trailing behind, the whole of the party collecting in an open space in front of us. They were about to begin, we were told, their famous buffalo dance. First round and round they tramped with measured steps, then they rushed against each other, then separated, then again met. Some were overthrown, but quickly getting on their feet, rejoined their companions. Now they bent down on all fours; now one buffalo, seizing a bow, shot a blunt arrow at another. Some had shields and spears; some, mounted on the backs of their companions, charged at everyone they met; all the time the whole band were stamping, bellowing, yelping, and making other terrific noises, while another party were seated on the ground beating their drums, and shaking their rattles, the dancers keeping time to the discordant music. It is difficult to describe the feats of the different performers, for each man appeared to dance until he could dance no more, except that when a pretended buffalo was shot by a blunt arrow, he was dragged out, and another immediately took his place.

This amusement went on until we were utterly weary of witnessing it, though at first it was amusing enough. I then suggested to Yellow Wolf that he should order the dancers to " knock off;" but he replied that the efficacy of the ceremony depended upon its continuing until the buffalo should appear.

" But suppose they should not come for a whole moon, your braves will be pretty well worn out by that time," I remarked.

" But they will come before then," he answered.

" So I should hope," I said, laughing.

At last a bevy of squaws placed on the ground, in front of the tent, an abundant feast of various messes, of which our host invited us to partake, suggesting that we should add a few articles from our own stores, including a bottle of fire-water, " for which," he observed, " his lips felt a peculiar longing."

We took the hint, but Dick ordered only a small bottle to be brought, observing that we kept the fire-water for sick men, or for such occasions as the present, and that we could not venture to draw largely on our store.

Unattractive as were the dishes the Redskin damsels offered us, they were far more palatable than might have been expected.

As the Indians liked their own dishes best, and we preferred ours, we did not trespass very largely on theirs. We found from the small amount of meat in the village, that the inhabitants were more hard up for food than we had supposed.

The buffalo dancers all the time continued their performance, being evidently impressed with the belief that the more furiously they danced, the sooner the buffaloes would make their appearance. Night brought no cessation, one relay of performers relieving the other without intermission; so that I was afraid poor Charley would have but little chance of a sleep. He, however, when I paid him a visit before retiring, assured me that he had got accustomed to the noise; and that the Flower of the Prairies had taken such good care of him that he was perfectly ready to remain where he was. Although we had every confidence in the honesty of our new friends, we deemed it prudent to keep a watch at night, both in camp and over the animals, for fear some young brave might take it into his head to distinguish himself by running off with a horse or two, as he would be sure to find a welcome among any friendly tribe, after the performance of such an act. I have no doubt there are some noble Redskins fit to become heroes of romances; but the greater part are unmitigated savages, with notions of right and wrong very different from those of civilized people.

The next day we paid a visit to Yellow Wolf, when we found his people still dancing with unabated vigour.

"The buffalo have not come yet!" I observed to him.

"Wait a bit, they come by-and-by," he replied. Dick suggested that we should strike away westward in search of them, but Yellow Wolf replied that it would be of no use, and that probably the buffalo would turn back and take a different course, should the pale-faces pursue them.

Old Ben advised us not to act contrary to the chief's wishes, observing that he undoubtedly had a very correct notion of when the buffalo would appear, as he never allowed the dance to commence until he calculated that the herd were not far off.

Wishing to cement our friendship with the chief

THE INDIAN "BUFFALO DANCE."

we invited him and some of his principal braves to
our camp, where we provided a feast as suitable to
their tastes as we were capable of producing. They
approved of the boiled ham and pork as well as the
corn cakes, sweetened with sugar, which old Ben
manufactured; but they hinted pretty strongly that
the stuff our flasks contained was more to their taste
than anything else we possessed. We took good
care, however, not to give them enough to make them
drunk; but Armitage observed that we were doing
them harm by creating in them a taste for spirits, and
that it would have been wiser not to allow them from
the first to know that we had any.

The feast was over, and our guests were smoking
the tobacco with which we provided them, puffing
away with evident enjoyment, when a young brave
was seen galloping towards our camp at headlong
speed. As he approached, he cried out,—

" The buffalo! the buffalo are coming!"

" I said so!" exclaimed Yellow Wolf, springing up
and rushing towards his horse. We all followed his
example, leaving Pierre and the Indians in charge of
the camp.

Yellow Wolf and his followers directed their course
towards their lodges to obtain their bows and arrows;
for, to show the confidence they placed in us, they
had come without them. As we came near, we saw,
far to the north and north-west, the whole ground
covered with a dark mass of shaggy monsters, tossing
their heads and flourishing their tails, the ground
literally trembling beneath their feet as they dashed
on towards us. The course they were following

THE BUFFALO CHARGING THE CAMP.

would bring them directly down upon the camp. We might as well have endeavoured to stop a cataract as to have tried to turn them aside. Their sudden ap·pearance caused the greatest excitement and confusion in the camp. The buffalo dancers, who had danced they were convinced to some purpose, having thrown off their masquerading dresses, were rushing here and there to obtain their arms and catch their horses. Before, however, the greater number were ready for the encounter, the buffalo were in their midst; and, to the dismay of the inmates, charged right through the camp, capsizing wigwams, trampling over women and children, dashing through the fires, and crushing pots and pans. Many of the brutes, however, paid dearly for their exploit; as the hunters, with shouts and shrieks, followed them up, shooting down some, spearing others, and hamstringing the brutes right and left, who were too much astonished and confused at the unexpected reception they met with to escape. I made my way to the chief's wigwam, which I was thankful to see still standing, and was just in time to shoot a buffalo charging at it with a force which would have upset a structure of ten times its stability. As it was, the animal rolled over, close to the tent poles. It was the first buffalo I had killed, and I was the prouder of the exploit as I had saved Charlie and the Flower of the Prairies from injury. I saw the chief galloping after another buffalo charging an old warrior fallen to the ground, and who would, in another moment, have been trans·fixed by its horns, had not Yellow Wolf stuck his spear behind its shoulder so powerful a blow that the creature rolled over, not, however, without almost crushing the old man's legs. The fierce onslaught made by the Indians on the herd at length divided it, some of the animals going off to the south-east, others to the south-west. Greatly to our satisfaction they then passed by on either side of our camp, several of their number being brought down by Ben Folkard's and Pierre's unerring rifles, three also being killed by our Indian followers. We, as well as the Indians, however, excited by the chase, still followed the buffaloes, although it seemed to me that we had already as much meat as the people could possibly consume.

Away we went, the Indians pursuing the cows, which they had singled out, their flesh being of the most value, though they were much smaller than the bulls. I confess, as they were all galloping along together, that I could scarcely distinguish one from the other. I found myself at length alone, pursuing part of the herd which had turned away eastward. I had managed to knock over two animals, and having again loaded made chase after a cow which had sepa-rated from her companions, I being determined to shoot her and then return. For some time she gave me no chance, as, unless I could obtain a broad-side shot, there was no use in firing. My horse was beginning to get blown, but I urged him on with whip and spur, until at length I managed to get up to within a few paces, when rising in my stirrups I fired down upon the animal. It seemed like the work of a moment, scarcely had I pulled the trigger than down dropped the buffalo, the bullet having broken her

[p. 100.

"DOWN HE CAME, ALMOST UPON ME"

spine. So rapid was the pace of my horse, that he was unable to stop himself. He made an attempt, however, to spring over the buffalo, but his feet striking its body over he rolled sending me with my gun still grasped in my hand, flying to the opposite side, when down he came almost upon me. At first I was seized with the dreadful idea that both my legs were broken, and I expected that my horse in his struggles would crush me still further, but the well-trained creature, recovering himself, rose to his feet without trampling upon me. Fortunately my sword was not broken, nor thrown out of the scabbard.

For some time I lay holding his bridle but unable to move. I was far away from either of my companions and was much afraid that I should not be discovered. The first thing I had to do was to try and get into my saddle; but, should I fail, dreadful might be my fate. My horse might perhaps make his way into camp, and by his appearance show that some accident had happened to me. I had a pocket-book and tore out a leaf and wrote—"Lying on the ground with both legs broken, to the eastward of the camp," and signed it, "Tom Rushforth."

I endeavoured to reach one of my stirrups to which I intended to fasten the paper and then to set my horse at liberty. Before doing so, however, I thought I would examine my legs and ascertain if they were really broken. On feeling the bones, to my infinite satisfaction I could discover no fracture, though they pained me greatly. I accordingly tried and succeeded in getting up; and, although I do not think I could have walked a yard, I managed to scramble into my saddle with my gun. I then, having thrown down a handkerchief to mark the cow I had shot as my own, put my horse's head, as I supposed, in the direction of the camp.

I was anxious to get back as soon as possible, but the pain of riding fast was greater than I could bear, and I was compelled to make my horse walk at a pace not suited to his fancy.

I could still see the buffalo scampering over the prairie, moving off to the southward, and I concluded that they would be miles away before the end of the day. I looked round for any friends, but not a horseman could I discover.

The weather had been bright during the early part of the day, but clouds were now drifting rapidly over the sky, and I continued riding on towards the north-west until the sun became totally obscured. I still believed that I could direct my course right. To trot was unbearable, but I thought that I might venture on a gallop; the movement, however, caused me so much pain that I was compelled again to pull up. In vain my eyes ranged over the wide extent of the prairie, in search of the wigwams of our Indian friends. For some time I guided myself by the wind, but that also shifted and fell light, so that I was unable to steer by it. I could distinguish the trail of the buffalo, by the tall grass which they had trampled down; but that did not serve to guide me, for it seemed to bend in all directions, though I have no doubt it would have served an Indian perfectly. I arrived at length at the unpleasant conclusion, that I had lost myself; still, could I but get a gleam of sunshine, or see the distant hills, I might, I hoped, ascertain what direction to take.

Had I not been so severely injured, I should not have cared so much; for having just before taken a good meal, I could have gone without food until the following day. I felt sure that my friends would come to search for me, but it might be long before I should be discovered, and the pain I suffered warned me of the importance of getting into camp as soon as possible.

My rifle was loaded, and I fired it off two or three times, hoping that the sound might be heard. I listened eagerly expecting a reply. A perfect silence, however, reigned over the vast plain. At length I became seriously anxious about my safety. I was still convinced that I was riding towards the west, and I pushed on. From the feeling in my legs, I fancied they must have swelled to twice their natural size, but on looking down they appeared as usual. The pain caused my spirits to sink, and all sorts of gloomy thoughts passed through my mind. Again and again I looked round. At length I saw in the far distance, an object moving over the plain, which I at once conjectured was a horseman, though I could only distinguish the upper part of his body. I turned my horse's head towards him, and raised my rifle in the air, hoping that he might perceive it. As I got nearer, I saw, by the plume on his head, that he was an Indian, and I naturally concluded that he was either Yellow Wolf or one of his braves, or perhaps one of our own people. I was somewhat surprised, however, when instead of coming on directly towards me, he turned to the right, and began to move on at a gallop over the ground. I then perceived that his head-dress was different to that of my friends, and that he carried a long shield and spear, as well as a bow and arrows. I had just reached a slight knoll, on which I pulled up that I might the more carefully survey the stranger. An attentive look at him convinced me that he was a Coomanche, one of the same people who had before attacked us, so that I knew I must treat him as an enemy rather than a friend. Should I let him get near me, I felt pretty sure that, if he was a Coomanche, he would play me some treacherous trick. I therefore unslung my rifle, and in a loud voice shouted to him to keep his distance.

He heard me clearly enough, but instead of stopping galloping towards me, he threw himself on the side of his horse, and, before I could cover him with my rifle, I saw the head of an arrow projecting over his saddle. To avoid it by retreating was impossible, so, bringing my rifle up to my shoulder, I gave a sudden jerk to my rein, which made my horse step back a few paces, and the arrow, aimed at my body, flew by in front of his nose. I had refrained from firing. The Coomanche, for such I concluded that he was, seeing that he was in my power—having shot another arrow which in his flurry, he was prevented aiming truly—galloped off to a distance.

I now shouted to him, threatening to kill his horse, and advising him to take himself off. He seemed doubtful, apparently, what to do. He might have hoped, that, should I execute my threat, he might still bring me down with an arrow, and by mounting my steed make his escape; but he must have been well aware there are many chances in warfare, and that I might shoot him instead of his steed. He might have guessed, by my not having fired, that I had my wits about me. I of course narrowly watched his movements, and seeing him glance over his shoulder, the idea occurred to me, that he was expecting others of his tribe to appear, in which case I should have but little chance of escaping.

At length he decided how to act. Once more he made at me, shooting a couple of arrows in rapid succession. One went through the sleeve of my coat; another struck the saddle, narrowly missing my legs, but did not pierce through the leather.

He might have half-a-dozen more arrows in his hand, and it was necessary to be cautious. As he circled round, I kept turning so as always to face him, when he was afraid of riding directly at me, for should he do so, he would he knew inevitably expose himself, and I should scarcely fail to miss him. His object was, I concluded, to keep me employed until the arrival of his friends. It would be folly to do as he wished. As long as I remained on the same spot, I could at any moment take a steady aim at him. Though he was aware of this, he trusted to my not firing, for fear of being unarmed should he charge me. At length he came so near, that I resolved not to lose the opportunity of knocking over his horse. I aimed just behind the animal's shoulder, and must have shot it through the heart; for, giving one bound, it fell over dead. The active Indian, however, in a moment

"AS HE CIRCLED ROUND, I KEPT TURNING SO AS ALWAYS
TO FACE HIM."

extricating himself, leapt to his feet, and came bounding towards me.

In a moment my trusty sword was out of its sheath, when, with a howl of disappointed rage, the Coomanche, seeing it uplifted to cut him down, turned tail and ran off as fast as his legs would carry him. I immediately reloaded and should, I believe, have shot the Redskin also ; but I had no wish to take the poor wretch's life, though, for my own safety, I determined to do so, should he again approach me. At that moment, the sun coming out from behind a cloud, just above the horizon, shone on a distant peak, which I had remarked from our camp. I had now no doubt as to the direction I should take. In spite of the agony the movement caused me, I put my horse into a gallop, leaving my late antagonist to pursue his way unhindered, and steered my course towards the northwest, where I hoped before long to discover my friends. The sun, however, sunk before I had seen either them or the Indian wigwams. Still the glow in the western sky guided me long after darkness had crept over the open prairie. When that disappeared, I was again at a loss how to keep a straight course. Throwing therefore the reins on my horse's neck, I trusted to his instinct to lead me aright.

I had gone on for two hours in the darkness when, to my joy, I saw a bright light ahead. It was that, I had little doubt, of our own camp fire. I was not mistaken. In a short time Dick's cheery voice welcomed me. He and my other companions had become anxious at my non-appearance. I was almost falling from my horse, and could not have dismounted with-

out assistance.   On telling them of my fight with the
Coomanche, Pierre immediately sent off to tell our
Indian friends of my suspicions that a party of their
enemies were in the neighbourhood.

CHAPTER VI.

BEING fully satisfied that the Shianees would prove
friendly and staunch, we agreed to move our camp
close to theirs, that we might the better be able to
withstand any attack which the Coomanches might
venture to make upon us. I managed, with the
assistance of my friends, to mount my horse so as to
perform the short journey, though I suffered a considerable amount of pain. We found Yellow Wolf
and his braves seated in council, to decide on a plan
of operations against the enemy. He expressed his
gratitude for the warning I had given him, and complimented me on the victory I had obtained over the
Coomanche brave. " Scouts have been sent out," he
said, " to ascertain the position of the enemy, but as
yet no information has been received of their whereabouts." He suspected that they were very numerous, or they would not have ventured into that part
of the country; but with our assistance he had no
doubt about his being able to repel an attack. Had
his tribe been alone he would have moved westward
to escape from them, as his object at present was to
kill buffalo, and lay in a winter store of pemmican.

There was little sleep for any of the party that night. The Indians were preparing to set out on the war-path, while my companions sat up not knowing at what moment the Coomanches might burst upon us, and I was kept awake by the pain my legs continued to cause me. Yellow Wolf, on seeing how much I suffered, sent his wife over with a supply of salves to doctor me.

The night, however, passed away in quietness; and when the scouts returned in the morning they reported that they had been unable to discover any traces of an enemy. We therefore remained in camp, both for my sake, and Charley's; while all hands were employed in manufacturing pemmican. The rest, and the care bestowed upon me by the Flower of the Prairies, had so beneficial an effect that in the course of a couple of days I was myself again.

I should have said that the Indians had brought in the meat from the cow and two bulls I had killed, having discovered them in the direction I had described. The flesh of the buffaloes having by this time been cut up and turned into pemmican, no small portion having been eaten by the Indians, both they and we were ready to recommence our march.

Just as we were about to start, a scout brought word that he had discovered a Coomanche trail, but being alone he was afraid to follow it up. The chief rated him soundly for his cowardice, and declared his intention of setting out himself with one of his braves, to learn what he could from an inspection of the enemy's position, so as to be able as far as possible

"YELLOW WOLF LED, AND HIS BRAVE FOLLOWED."   [p. 113.

to judge of their intended movements.   I volunteered to accompany him.

" There are few pale-faces from whom I would accept such an offer," he answered ; "but you have shown so much courage and discretion, that I shall be glad of your company."

I do not mean to say that he used these words, but it was something equivalent.   I thanked him for the compliment, which I modestly remarked was scarcely deserved.   Dick and Armitage strongly advised me not to go ; but, having made the offer, I felt I should lose credit with the Redskins should I draw back. We were to proceed with three mounted attendants, who were to take charge of our steeds as we drew near the enemy's camp, and we were then to go forward on foot.

" We may have to run for our lives should we be discovered," said Yellow Wolf, as we rode along; " and unless you can depend upon your legs, it will be wise to remain with the horses."

I replied that my object was to see the way of approaching an enemy's camp, and to get a sight of it, and that I felt sure I could run as fast as he could. We accordingly continued on until we came upon the trail which the scout had discovered.   Yellow Wolf now proceeded more cautiously, it being of the greatest importance that the enemy should not dis-cover us.   At length he announced his belief that we had got near the Coomanche camp.   We therefore left our horses in charge of the three Indians, and then continued in the direction we were before going on foot.   I observed that Yellow Wolf's eye ranged over the ground on either side, as well as ahead. As I thought of the distance we had come since we left our horses, I began to repent somewhat of the task I had undertaken; however, I trusted to the sagacity of my companion, that we should not be detected, and that we should be able to retreat as we had advanced. Yellow Wolf led, and his brave followed, I bringing up the rear. My companions frequently stopped, and, bending their ears to the ground, listened for any sounds which might warn them they were reaching the Coomanche camp. At first they walked upright, but now they bent down, taking advantage of any cover which offered.

At length they stopped and whispered together, and Yellow Wolf told me to be more careful than ever. Then again he and his companion moved on, until he made a sign to me to keep under cover, while they crept forward along the top of a bank, covered by bushes of wild roses. I saw them eagerly stretching out their necks, so as to obtain a view beyond. I crept after them, looking through the bushes, and could distinguish in the plain below a considerable band of warriors, some engaged in lighting fires, others in collecting wood, or preparing provisions, while their horses ranged round near at hand.

It would have been a fine opportunity to take them by surprise, for a mounted party could have swept down upon them before they had time to catch their horses. I have no doubt the Yellow Wolf thought the same thing, but neither he nor his companion uttered a word.

After satisfying my curiosity, I crept back as cautiously as I had advanced; and the two Indians, who had surveyed the camp to their satisfaction, came after me. We at once commenced a retreat in the same fashion as we had advanced, being quite as careful to conceal ourselves. Their great object was to escape detection, so that their enemies might not be aware that the position of their camp was known, and might continue as unprepared for the reception of a foe as they appeared to be at present.

Not until we regained our horses, did the Yellow Wolf speak. As we galloped along on our return, he told me that the Coomanches would remain at their present camp for a couple of days, and would then proceed to the north-west in the hopes of coming up with the herds of buffalo which were feeding in that direction. How he knew this is more than I can say. I asked him whether he intended to attack the Coomanches.

He replied that he must hold a council with his braves, and that if they agreed to follow him, he proposed doing so the next morning in the hopes of catching his foes off their guard. He inquired whether I and my friends would assist. I replied that I could not give an answer without consulting them; that we had come to the country, not to make war on the Redskins, and that it was our practice to fight only when we were attacked. This answer did not appear particularly to please him. I said, however, that should he and his people be attacked, we would no doubt fulfil our promise in assisting them.

"The pale-faces are wise," he remarked, "they

fight only when they are obliged; that is the reason why red man go down and they live."

Great excitement was produced in the camp by the news we brought, and without loss of time a council was held. I told my friends what Yellow Wolf had said, but they decided at once not to assist him in attacking the Coomanche camp. "We shall have quite enough to do in making our way through the country, without joining in quarrels not our own," observed Armitage.

We waited with some anxiety, therefore, the result of our friends' deliberations. At last Yellow Wolf came to our camp and announced that his braves were unanimous in their resolution of attacking the Coomanches; that they intended to set out that night so as to surprise them just before daybreak. He invited us to accompany them; when Dick, getting up, made him a speech in true Indian fashion, expressing our gratitude for the treatment Charley and I had received from the " Flower of the Prairies," and our affection for him and his; but at the same time observing that we must decline to cut the throats of a number of people with whom we had no quarrel.

The chief, who took our refusal very good-humouredly, asked if we would assist in guarding the camp and the women and children during his absence. This request we could not well refuse, and we had therefore to agree to await his return, Dick telling him that we hoped he would come back victorious.

This matter settled, he and his braves immediately set out; while we kept a strict watch on the camp, which we thought it more than probable might be attacked during the absence of the warriors whose departure their cunning enemies might have discovered.

Although there were two or three alarms caused by a pack of cayotes which approached the camp, the morning broke without an enemy having been seen. We had still many hours to wait the result of the battle. It was not until near the evening that a band of horsemen were seen approaching from the northeast. They might be friends or they might be enemies. We all hastened to our posts, old men and boys seizing their arms ready to fight if necessary. As the horsemen drew nearer, the Indians uttered loud cries of satisfaction, for they were discovered to be their friends. Still they came on slowly. It appeared to me that their numbers were diminished. Presently Yellow Wolf dashed forward bearing a couple of scalps at the end of his spear. Other braves followed, several of them having the same gory trophies. On getting up close to the camp, they halted to receive the congratulations of their friends.

The old men and women then began to inquire for the relatives who were no longer among them. The same answer was given to all, " He fell fighting bravely." On hearing this, loud wails arose from those who had lost husbands, brothers, and sons.

It was some time before we could learn from Yellow Wolf what had happened. He had been entirely successful in surprising the Coomanche camp, but they had fought desperately and many of his braves fell before he had succeeded in putting his enemies to flight. The scalps he had brought showed the

number of slain on the other side. Another day was lost, while our savage friends blackened their faces and mourned for the dead, after which they danced their hideous scalp-dance. I was thankful that they had returned without prisoners; for I am certain they would have put them to death with all sorts of horrible tortures, even though we might have protested against so barbarous a custom. They, however, managed to bring back one of their people desperately wounded, with two arrows and a bullet through his body. It seemed surprising that he could have lived so long. It was, however, evident to us that he was dying; but his friends thought that he might be recovered by the efforts of one of their medicine-men, whose vocation we had not before discovered. The patient was laid on the ground half-stripped, while the tribe sat round in a circle. Presently, from out of one of the tents, the most grotesque figure I ever beheld made his appearance. A huge wolf-skin cloak covered his back; on his head he wore a mask, representing the head of a wolf double the ordinary size. Dried frogs and fish and snakes hung down from his neck, his whole body being concealed by skins. In one hand he carried a spear, ornamented with a variety of coloured feathers and snakes twisting up it, and in the other a sort of tambourine, from which also were hung snakes and frog-skins. He advanced, making a series of jumps and uttering wild yells accompanied by the rattling of his magic drum until, entering the circle, he approached his patient He then began to dance round him, striking and rattling his drum, shrieking and shouting; sometimes leaping over the wounded man, then shaking him from side to side.

I watched the poor sufferer, who endured the fearful pain to which he was put without a groan, gazing at the hideous figure, the last sight he was destined to behold on earth; for in a short time his jaw fell, his eyes became fixed, and he was dead. Still the conjurer, utterly unconscious of this, went on with his performance; until at length his eye falling on the body and perceiving what had occurred, he turned round and darted into his tent. The Indians did not appear to be very much surprised, but I suppose fancied that they had done their best for their friend, and that their medicine-man had done all that he could do to save the life of the brave.

As Charley was now sufficiently recovered to move, Armitage proposed that we should recommence our march, and we prepared accordingly. Our new friends, however, were not so easily to be shaken off, and when they discovered our intentions, they made preparations to accompany us.

I have not described their lodges. They were of a conical form, the frame-work of straight long poles about twenty-five feet long. This was first erected, when round it were stretched a number of well-dressed buffalo robes, sewn tightly together and perfectly water-proof. The point where the ends of the poles protruded was left open to allow the smoke to escape. On one side was the entrance closed by a door, also of buffalo hide. The fire was made in the centre, immediately under the aperture. In cold weather the Indians slept on buffalo rugs, with their feet towards the fire, and these rugs were rolled up during the day and placed at the back of the lodge.

The women had all the work of putting up the lodges. We watched the poor creatures taking them down again, rolling up the skins, and placing them on bars near the lower ends of the poles, which trailed on the ground, the upper ends being secured half on each side of the horses. The young squaws and children were mounted on the horses, while the older had to toil along on foot often with loads on their backs. Besides horses, our friends had a number of dogs which were employed in drawing loads on small sledges, and very hard work they must have found it in summer. They had also other dogs of a smaller species which were reserved for food when buffalo meat was not to be obtained.

For three days we travelled on in their company, when the scouts brought word that a large herd of buffaloes were feeding a few leagues off to the southwest. Our friends immediately encamped and prepared to set off in chase, trusting that the Coomanches, after the signal defeat they had received, would not attack them. We should have been glad of an excuse for separating from our friends; but as we wished to see more of their mode of hunting the buffalo, we agreed to accompany them. Charley, I was glad to see, was as well able to sit his horse as before, and he declared that he was ready to undergo any amount of fatigue. According to our custom, we kept as much together as possible; but we endeavoured not to show that we doubted the honest intentions of the Indians.

Occasionally the Yellow Wolf, getting off his horse, put his ear to the ground to listen, as he said "for the feet of the buffalo."

At length, quickly mounting, he exclaimed that he heard them and that we should soon come in sight of the herd. We therefore pushed rapidly forward; and, reaching the top of a slight rising, we saw a large number of black dots scattered over the plain. To the right, on one side of where the buffalo were feeding, was a smaller elevation to that on which we were posted. Guided by the chief we made towards it. On reaching the further or western side, the chief advised that we should dismount, saying that he wished to attack the buffalo in a way often adopted by his people before charging in among them on horseback. We of course agreed, anxious to see the method he spoke of.

The Indians had brought with them several wolf-skins with the heads and tails. Creeping up the hill, over the brow of which we looked to watch what was going forward, we saw them put the skins on their backs, and take their bows and a quantity of arrows in their hands, so that at a distance they much resembled wolves. On they went, whenever shelter could be obtained, running rapidly forward, but as they got on the open plain again bending down and creeping on all fours. Whenever they saw the shaggy beasts looking at them, they stopped and seemed to be engaged with something on the ground, as if they had no intention of approaching the herd. When the buffaloes went on feeding they again advanced.

Were the buffaloes sharp-sighted animals they

might have discovered their foes; but their hair covering their eyes prevents them from seeing clearly. The hunters got closer and closer.

Having selected the fattest animal in sight, presently one, rising for a moment, let fly his arrow, which entered the breast of a buffalo near him. The animal, after running for a few paces, dropped without disturbing the rest, who seemed to fancy that their companion had merely lain down on the ground. Each of the other Indians did the same, and, without taking any notice of the beasts they had killed, continued their course, shooting arrow after arrow, until upwards of a dozen buffaloes had bit the ground.

It is only, however, when the bison are quietly feeding that they can be approached in this way. When they are on the move, they keep their eyes about them, and a man on foot can with difficulty get near. The disguised hunters would probably have killed many more, but that for some reason or other the herd began to move on. The moment the chief observed this he called to us and the others to come forward; and away we dashed after the herd, which, alarmed at the sound of the horses' hoofs, rushed on, every instant increasing their speed. As before all was silence and quiet, now the air was rent with a confusion of sounds—the tramp of the bisons and the pursuing horses, the shouts and cries of the hunters as they dashed forward in chase.

We let them take the lead for some time, to see their mode of proceeding. We remarked especially the force and precision with which, while going at full gallop, they let fly their arrows, always aiming behind the shoulders of the shaggy beasts. They took good care never to head them, while they kept at a sufficient distance to have room to avoid the fierce charges the terror-stricken bisons occasionally made.

After they had shot a considerable number, we who had hitherto kept in the rear gave our horses the rein and were soon up with the herd.

Armitage and Story were in their glory, and upheld the honour of the white man by each shooting three buffaloes, while Dick and I killed two. I saw Charley shoot down one in very good style, and then pursue another which he had made up his mind to overtake. I was on the point of following him, when my horse stumbled in a hole and threw me over its head. I quickly recovered my feet and was about to remount, my steed appearing none the worse for its fall, when I saw a huge buffalo dashing up with the intention of tossing me into the air. I had barely time to spring into my saddle and to get a few paces off, when the buffalo's horns pierced the ground at the very spot where I had been standing. Disappointed at not finding me, he looked about and again lowered his head to charge. Flight was my only resource; so off I galloped, hoping to get to such a distance from the brute as would allow me time to reload and again to face him. I succeeded better than I expected; and at length, wheeling round my horse who stood stock-still, I fired and brought the buffalo to the ground. In the meantime the rest of the herd galloped off followed by the hunters, who were now a long distance

away, so far indeed as to make it impossible for me
to overtake them. Well satisfied with my performance, I cut out the tongue of the last animal I had
killed and directed my course back to the camp,
stopping on my way to extract the tongues of the
two other bisons I had killed. I was soon overtaken
by Dick, who had also turned back. He said that
the rest of our party had gone on with the Indians, in
pursuit of the herd.

He regretted that Charley had not returned with
us, as he would be overcome with fatigue by so long
a ride. We employed ourselves in lighting a fire
and getting supper ready for our friends. At last
Armitage and Story came in, but Charley did not
make his appearance.

"He'll return soon," said Dick. "Let me consider, when did I see him last? I cannot quite recol-
lect, but I remember that he was following a buffalo;
and I had no doubt that he shot the brute, and fully
expected to see him here."

We waited, but we waited in vain. At last we
applied to our Indian friends, but they were revelling
in buffalo meat, and were not disposed to set out in
search of Charley; promising, however, to go in the
morning should the young pale-face not have returned
by that time.

I am afraid to say how much buffalo meat the
savages consumed before daybreak, for they sat up
nearly all night eating, and had their enemies pounced
down upon them they would have made but a poor
defence, I suspect.

When morning came they excused themselves from

INDIAN BUFFALO HUNT.

going in search of Charley, saying that they must bring in the buffalo meat they had killed.

We therefore had to set off alone, not a little disgusted at their behaviour. We bade them, however, a friendly farewell, saying that the life of one of our party was more precious to us than all the buffalo meat in the world. We however took with us the tongues and other portions of the animals we had killed, so that we had abundance of provisions which would last us until we could obtain venison or fall in with another herd of buffalo.

Though we made diligent search, with the assistance of old Folkard and the Indians engaged by Armitage, we failed to discover Charley's trail; and we felt more out of spirits when we encamped that evening than we had done during the whole of our expedition.

CHAPTER VII.

SEVERAL days were spent in a vain search for Charley. Armitage and Story said they feared that he must either have been killed by a buffalo, and his body devoured by wolves; or that he had been carried away by some small party of Indians who had been watching us, and had captured him, though afraid to attack our camp.

Both Dick and I, however, could not bring ourselves to believe that he was dead. We were glad to find that old Folkard was of our opinion. He had known men, he said, who had wandered away from camp and been absent several weeks before they were found or managed to make their way back themselves. Charley had a good supply of ammunition, and being a fair shot, would be able to procure food. We begged Armitage and Dick to remain in the locality some time longer. This they consented to do. We were now in the neighbourhood of the Rocky Mountains, where they might obtain a variety of sport, so that they had no cause to complain of their detention. My thoughts, as well as Dick's, were entirely occupied by Charley, and we could take no interest in

NARROW ESCAPE FROM A GRISLY. [p. 133.

hunting. We, however, did our duty in trying to supply the camp with game.

The chief part of our time was taken up in scouring the country in the hopes of discovering our young friend, or ascertaining the cause of his death.

At length the old trapper bade us farewell, saying that he should strike away north, to a district where beavers abounded, for he could no longer spend his time in comparative idleness. We were sorry to lose him, for he was a capital companion, especially round the camp fire, when he indulged us in his quaint way with his numberless adventures and hair-breadth escapes, sufficient to make the hair of my old uncle, the Alderman, stand out from his head.

Day after day went by. When we met Pierre and the Indians who had assisted us in the search, the same reply alone was forthcoming.

"You see, it is hopeless," said Jack to Dick Buntin. "Your young friend must have lost his life. I am very sorry, but we must be moving westward. It won't do to detain Armitage longer. He is very good-natured, but from what he said to me yesterday, he will be starting away without us. He requires action. He is not happy, I suspect, from something which took place between him and Ellen Hargrave, so that we must decide what to do."

Dick pleaded hard for another day, still persisting in his belief that we should find Charley. Our Indian friends had promised should they discover any traces of him to send us word, but nothing had been heard from them.

Dick and I had made a longer expedition than

usual, and returned so tired, that the next morning we were utterly unable to set out. A day's rest would, however, we thought, restore our strength. Towards the evening, while the remainder of the party were still away, Dick walked to a shady spot some distance from the camp, taking a large buffalo robe to lie upon, with a book, his pipe and gun.

One of the Indians who had remained with us, had meantime made up a fire. I saw at length by my watch, that it was time to prepare for supper, and as Dick still acted as cook, I sent the Indian to summon him. The man had not gone long, when I heard him shout. Fearing that something was the matter, I hurried forward, when what was my dismay to see a huge grisly standing on its hind legs, as if about to make its last fatal spring, close to Dick, who had no weapon in his hand with which to defend himself. I had brought my gun, but dared not fire for fear of killing my friend instead of the bear. Dick, however, seemed in no way dismayed, and as I got a little nearer, I saw that he held a large buffalo robe in both his hands. The Indian and I shouted in the hopes of distracting Bruin's attention. Our cries were responded to by Armitage and Story, who at that moment providentially made their appearance. Still none of us dared to fire, though we approached nearer and nearer, hoping that the bear would postpone his spring until we could get near enough to shoot him through the head without injuring our friend. Presently the bear growling savagely, indicative of his intention to seize his victim, began to advance; when Dick, who had never for a moment withdrawn his eyes from the monster, in an instant threw the cloak over its head. He then springing back, ran off as hard as his legs could carry him, his example being imitated by the Indians. The bear in its struggles drew the cloak close over its eyes, when I fired and over it rolled with its legs in the air. Still it was not dead, and might at any moment be up again; and, more savage than ever from its wound, would be certain to attack us fiercely.

Armitage and Story, making their way through the brushwood, had now got near enough to fire. They pulled their triggers at the same moment, while I quickly reloaded. It was fortunate that I did so, for notwithstanding its wounds, the bear, suddenly regaining its feet, made a dash at me who was nearest to it, and in another instant I should have been torn by its tremendous claws, when I fired and to my infinite satisfaction it again rolled over and, giving another convulsive struggle, lay dead.

Dick thanked us for our timely assistance, and promised that he would never as long as he lived go to sleep away from the camp in a region infested by grislies.

This was the first we had seen for some time, and the adventure was a caution to us to look out for them in future. With great reluctance on the part of Dick and me, we once more packed up and moved westward; still we did not abandon all hope that we should find our young friend. I, however, had lost the interest I had before felt in hunting, and would rather have gone back and contented myself with less exciting sport in one of the eastern states. As things turned out, it would have been better for all of us had we done so.

We made a good show as we rode over the prairie, with our baggage mules, our led horses, mounted Indians, our Canadian guide and our four selves; so that no ordinary band of Redskins was likely to attack our party, unless they could take us by surprise, and against that it was our constant care effectually to guard by keeping a bright look-out during the day, and a careful watch over the camp at night. Our Indians knew very well that they would be the first victims should we be attacked.

We were sure, in the neighbourhood of the Rocky Mountains which we had now reached, to fall in with big-horns, elks and antelopes, as well as buffalo in the lower ground. We accordingly encamped in a beautiful spot with the lofty mountains rising above us, while below extended the prairie far away to the horizon. I must not stop to describe our various adventures. Dick continued indifferent to sport, but occasionally went out with me; while Armitage and Story shot together, and never returned without a big-horn or two, or an elk. One day they appeared leading or rather dragging along what looked like a mass of shaggy fur of a tawny colour. As they approached, I saw that their captive was a young bear, with its head thoroughly covered up with the skin of another animal of the same description. They were laughing heartily, and every now and then springing forward to avoid the rushes made at them by the little creature. On finding all its efforts vain, it at length stopped, and refused to move. They told me that they had shot the mother and then one of her cubs ; that the other refusing to leave the body of its parent, they had time to take off the skin from the cub they had killed and had adroitly thrown it over the head of its brother, and that having a coil of rope they had managed to secure it. We hoped to tame our captive, but the moment the skin was taken off its head, darting at Jack, it gave him a severe bite in the leg, and nearly treated Armitage in the same manner, but fortunately he had a thick stick with which he gave the little brute so severe a blow on the nose, that it lay down, as we thought, in the sulks. We managed to tether it in a way effectually to prevent its escape, but the next morning we found, to our disappointment, that it was dead. The skins of the two animals were beautiful, their fur being very thick and long, and of a brown colour, with a stripe of darker hue along the back.

Next day our friends having again set out, I was endeavouring to persuade Dick to accompany me in another direction, when one of the Indians brought word that a herd of buffalo were feeding in the plain below. I should have said that the country was beautiful in the extreme, with thick woods of cedar and rhododendron covering it in all directions. The forests were, however, easily traversed, as paths were made through them by the buffalo and elk, who following each other's footsteps, had opened up bridle roads to all points of the compass. Feeling ashamed of not adding something to our store of provisions, when Dick declined accompanying me on the plea of not being up to work, I mounted my horse, and set

A LEAP IN TIME.

p. 139

off alone, hoping to shoot a buffalo before going far. I soon came in sight of a couple of herds, one of cows and another of bulls. Most of the former were followed by calves and were out of condition, but seeing some fat animals among them, I made chase. When the cows began to run they were joined by the bulls, and the whole set off together, scampering along at a tremendous rate. I kept the fat cows in sight, however, as away they went. Lightly built and more active than the bulls, they took the lead. At length I was getting up with one of the former which I had singled out, when a big bull, blown by his unusual exercise, halted just between me and the cow, and lowering his head prepared to charge, when his horns would in an instant have ripped open the breast of my noble steed. As I saw it about to charge, a thought occurred to me. Holding my gun in my left hand, and giving my horse the rein, I bestowed a tremendous cut with my heavy riding-whip on his flanks, which made him spring to a height sufficient to have cleared a five-barred gate; and when the bull rushed forward, over its back he went, clearing it in the most beautiful style, his hinder feet just grazing its shaggy hair. The next moment, instead of being rolled over on the ground, I found myself (though without my hat) safe on the other side; while the bull, not knowing what had become of me, dashed forward bellowing loudly in an opposite direction. A few more strides brought me close to the cow, when standing up in my stirrups I fired, and the animal instantly rolled over dead. I at once reloaded, and made chase after another, which I was also fortunate enough to kill. The rest of the herd made their escape. Satisfied with the result of my hunt, I dismounted and took possession of the tongues and marrow-bones, as well as some portions of the meat, intending to send the Indians back for the remainder, should the carcases have escaped the scent of the wolves. The buffalo meat was highly appreciated; indeed we lived like fighting cocks, and had every reason to expect to do so while we remained in that region. Pierre, however, advised that we should proceed, as some bands of hostile Indians were sure, before long, to find out that we were in the neighbourhood, and would take an opportunity of cutting us off when separated from each other should they not venture to attack our camp. Armitage and Jack were, however, inclined to laugh at Pierre's warnings. Jack too, who found his leg suffering from the bite that the little bear had given him, was disinclined to take a long journey. Dick, who had warned him from the first not to neglect the wound, took him under his care and insisted on his remaining quietly in camp for two or three days until he was well again. We employed the time in cleaning our arms, repairing our harness and clothes, and performing several other tasks such as the wear and tear of a hunter's life from time to time renders necessary. We had long discussions in camp as to what course we should pursue, Pierre advising that we should strike northward, and then take one of the passes through the Rocky Mountains generally followed by the emigrants to California.

Several days had passed away. Story was quite

recovered, and we were once more encamped, not much to Pierre's satisfaction, he declaring that we were still in a dangerous region, frequently visited by Apaches and other roving tribes, the deadly enemies of the pale-faces. Armitage and Story only laughed at his warnings, and even Dick felt much inclined to agree with them.

We had, as before, proceeded in three parties, one of the Indians having accompanied Armitage, and Jack and three others going with Pierre, while the rest remained with Dick and me in camp. Evening was approaching, and none of our friends had returned. Dick had sent out one of the Indians to see if they were coming, while he and I prepared the supper. In a short time the scout returned with a long face. He had caught sight, he said, of a large party of strange Redskins; who, not knowing that they were discovered, were making their way in the direction of our camp, evidently endeavouring to keep themselves concealed. He advised that we should gallop off on our horses, and leave our baggage and the other animals to their fate, as it would be impossible to defend the camp against so overwhelming a force. To this neither Dick nor I was inclined to agree, though of course it made us anxious for the arrival of our friends, when we hoped, by showing a bold front, to drive back the enemy.

We at once brought in our horses and mules, and tethered them in the rear of the camp; then calling on our Indians to assist us, we felled a couple of trees, which we placed so as to form a barricade in front.

It would afford us but a slight protection, but it was better than nothing.

We now looked out with more anxiety than ever for our friends, for they certainly ought to have returned to the camp some time before this. It was important not to be surprised, and knowing the stealthy way in which the savages were likely to approach, we were aware that any moment we might hear their fearful war-whoops, and find ourselves engaged in a desperate struggle for life. To prevent this, Dick proposed sending out the Indians to scout and ascertain the exact position of the enemy. They went more willingly than I should have supposed; but I remembered not being very well satisfied with the expression of their countenances. Dick and I were thus left alone in camp. To save ourselves from being shot down without warning, we took up our position behind the logs, with the spare rifles by our sides. Here we sat, expecting every moment the return of our Indians. We waited in vain. Darkness was coming on. Our position was indeed critical. If the savages, as reported by the scout, were in the neighbourhood, at any moment they might be down upon us. We now began to fear that our Indians had fallen into their hands. Perhaps, also, such might have been the fate of our friends. We had been sitting thus for an hour or more, and had become very hungry, when Dick proposed going to the fire to obtain some venison which had long been roasting there. He brought it, and I need not say that it was devoured with considerable satisfaction.

"Another piece won't do us any harm," I observed,

as I made my way towards the fire. I was returning, when what was my dismay to see half-a-dozen dark forms leap over the barricade and place themselves between Dick and me. I sprang towards our rifles, one of which Dick was in the act of grasping, to have a fight for life, when a savage knocking it out of his hand three others sprang upon him. The remainder throwing themselves upon me, we were in an instant prisoners. I fully expected the next moment to have my scalp taken off my head, and it was some satis-faction to find that it was allowed to remain on.

"1 hope the other fellows have escaped," said Dick; "we might, by giving a shout, warn them of their danger; and if Pierre joins them, they might manage to get hold of some of the horses."

As he spoke, he shouted at the top of his voice, and I joined him, crying out,—

"Keep away from the camp!"   •

No reply came. The Indians, instead of trying to stop us, only laughed; and, from the voices we heard around, we knew there must be many more of them.

Having bound our arms behind us, our captors sat themselves down to **examine** and consume the food we had provided for the rest of the party, and then proceeded to inspect the contents of our packs. While they were thus employed, a shout was raised, and shortly after another, when several Indians appeared, dragging Armitage and Jack along with them.

Still Pierre was at liberty; and we hoped that he might escape and give notice of our fate, or form some plan for our liberation. Great, therefore, was our disappointment when he too, shortly afterwards, was brought into camp. What had become of our Indians we could not tell. They had, we concluded, however, either been captured or deserted us.

Our captors, after a long consultation, carried us all a short distance from the camp to a clump of trees, to the trunks of which they bound us in a way which made it impossible to move either our arms or legs, when, having thus tied us up, they returned to our camp to examine and divide the spoil.

"We are in a bad case, I am afraid," said Armitage; "the savages have proved themselves more cunning than I had supposed, for they were upon Jack and me before we had time to lift our rifles to our shoulders."

"We might try to bribe them to let us off," I observed.

"Very little chance of their doing that; they'll help themselves to everything we possess, and won't trust to our promises," said Jack.

"They have the ugly custom of torturing prisoners before they kill them," said Dick. "I'm very glad Charley escaped our fate, poor fellow provided he hasn't met with a worse one."

I made no remark, though I was thinking all the time of various plans. I was anxious to hear what Pierre would say.

"Better tell them we English pale-faces," he observed at last; "dey kill us if dey like; but if dey do, our great Queen hunt up every man jack of dem, and hang dem."

I was very much inclined to agree with Pierre

that our best chance of escaping was to make the savages understand that we belonged to the pale-faces over the frontier, of whom they might possibly have heard, and that our Sovereign always punished those who injured her subjects.

The savages, however, at present, gave us no opportunity of addressing them; but we could see them unpacking our valises, pulling to pieces our well-made-up packs, overhauling our cooking utensils, apparently appropriating various articles, not, however, without a considerable amount of talking and gesticulation. They then put on our buffalo-meat and venison to cook, and began laughing and jeering at us as they ate it. At length they discovered several packages which had before escaped their notice, having been hidden in the grass. Among them was a case containing brandy; but as we kept it locked, it was some time before they managed to break it open with their axes. On finding that it contained bottles, they raised a shout of joy; and one being forthwith opened by knock-ing off the neck, the savage who had performed the operation poured some of the contents down his throat. Uttering a howl of satisfaction, he was about to take a second draught, when another seized it, and it was rapidly passed on, until it was empty. Another and another bottle was treated in the same way, although the chief of the party appeared to be urging his followers to take no more for the present; but to this they evidently did not agree; and while his back was turned, two more bottles were abstracted. On seeing this, he seized one of them, and poured no small part of the contents down his own throat, apparently fearing that his companions would drink it up and leave him none. The result which was to be expected followed; but they had swallowed the liquor too rapidly to render them immediately helpless, though it excited their fiercest passions; and to our horror, getting on their legs, they drew their tomahawks and approached us with the evident intention of taking our lives. Before, however, they had made many steps towards us, they sank to the ground; while others—with the bump of appropriativeness—took possession of all the goods within their reach. This was seen by the more sanguinarily disposed of the party, who turned their rage towards their companions, and, rushing on them, attempted to retake the articles they considered theirs. A fearful scuffle ensued: some, it appeared to us, were struck dead, or desperately wounded; but in the uncertain light afforded by the fire we could not exactly see what had happened. We could only make out that the whole party were quickly stretched on the ground, the victors and the vanquished lying side by side, including the chief, who appeared to be as helpless as the rest.

At length their shouts and groans were silenced. Not a sound reached our ears. Now was our opportunity; but in vain we endeavoured to break loose from our bonds. The savages had fastened them too securely to enable us to liberate ourselves. Dick made desperate efforts to reach with his mouth the rope which secured his arms.

"A FEARFUL STRUGGLE ENSUED."

"If I could but once get my teeth to it, I would soon bite it through," he exclaimed.

But again and again he tried to no purpose. We all followed his example, with the same result. In the morning, the savages would too probably recover, and revenge themselves on our heads for the death of their companions whom they themselves had killed. Hour after hour went by, and each brought us nearer to the moment that we must expect a fearful death.

CHAPTER VIII.

WE and the savage Redskins were both utterly helpless; they from being overcome by liquor, we from having our arms firmly bound to the trees. All the efforts we had made to liberate ourselves had only tended to draw more tightly the thongs; while we were left to contemplate the dreadful fate to which we were doomed as soon as the savages had recovered from the fumes of the spirits they had swallowed. All sorts of horrible ideas passed through my mind. Should a pack of wolves come to the camp, they might, helpless as we were, tear us to pieces, as well as the unconscious Indians. It would be a worse fate than any the savages might inflict upon us. Scarcely had the idea entered my brain, than the well-known howls and yelps of the animals I dreaded reached my ears. Louder and louder they grew. They were approaching the camp. In a few minutes they would be upon us. It was no fancy of my brain, for my companions heard them also. Darkness prevented us from seeing each other's countenances; but I could distinguish Dick, who was nearest me, again making efforts to free himself, and he could not help crying out in des-

peration when he found himseif foiled as before. The
wolves were close upon us, when presently we heard
the tramp of a horse's feet, and one of our own
animals, which either Armitage or Jack had been
riding, and from whose back the Indians had neg-

A RACE FOR LIFE.

lected to remove the saddle dashed by, closely pursued
by a pack of large wolves, who intent on the chase
did not regard us. I saw the head of an Indian
lifted up for a moment, awakened to partial consciousness by the yelping of the wolves and the
tramp of the horse ; but perhaps the savage fancied
he was dreaming, for the next moment his head again
sank to the ground. We were preserved for the
moment, but what would happen should the wolves
succeed in pulling down and devouring the horse ?

They would, to a certainty, return and attack us, as we had feared; or, even if they did not, the Indians would be recovering from their debauch. I could only hope that they had not consumed all the liquor, and that the first to awaken would take another pull at the bottles. In spite of our fearful position, a drowsiness began to steal over me, produced perhaps by exhaustion. I even now do not like to think of those dreadful hours, when my mind dwelt on the various tortures the savages were wont to inflict on their helpless prisoners. I fully expected that arrows would be shot at my limbs while all vital parts were avoided; to have my flesh burnt with hot irons; to be scalped; to suffer the most lingering and painful of deaths. In vain I tried to banish such thoughts, and to encourage the stupor stealing over me. At length I had almost succeeded, though I was not really asleep, when I heard a voice whisper in my ear, " Do not move or speak when you find the thongs cut."

The next instant I was free. The darkness prevented me seeing clearly what was happening to my companions, but I could distinguish a figure stealing along the ground, and appearing behind each of them.

" Now friends! you have your choice, either to cut the throats of the Redskins as they lie, or to catch the horses and put a wide space between them and yourselves before daybreak," said a voice which I recognised as that of old Folkard—" don't trust those villains, they may not be as fast asleep as you fancy. If they hear you moving they may be on their feet again before you have had time to pass your knives across their throats."

" Savages as they are, I would not for one moment dream of killing them, whatever they intended to do to us," said Jack.

Armitage and Story agreed with him, as did I. We therefore at once resolved to steal off as soon as we had recovered our rifles, the only weapons of which we had been deprived; and though they were close to where our captors were sleeping, they might easily be reached. Our plan was then to try and get hold of our horses, and when they were secured we might recover the remainder of our property and deprive the Indians of their arms. We should thus teach them a lesson of mercy; for when they recovered their senses they could not fail to see how completely they had been in our power, and that we might have put the whole of them to death had we been so disposed.

The old trapper volunteered to manage the most dangerous part of the undertaking, that of recovering our rifles. Telling us to remain where we were, apparently still bound to the trees, he crept forward on hands and knees, disappearing in the surrounding gloom. Not a sound did we hear until he came back, carrying in either hand a rifle, which he placed at our feet. He then made a second trip, which was as successful as the first; but the Indians' spears and several of our spare rifles had still to be obtained. He went very cautiously to work, for he was evidently not at all confident that one of the Indians might not awake. I would gladly have assisted him, had he not urged us to remain quiet. I felt greatly relieved when he at length returned with the last rifles.

" But we want our saddles!" whispered Dick.

I told Folkard where to find them.

" You shall have them," he answered, and again set off. I much feared that he might be discovered, as he would have to go into the camp itself, and the slightest sound might awaken our enemies.

We waited and waited : again I felt a strong inclination to steal forward and assist him. Just as I was about to do so, he reappeared bringing two saddles and bridles.

Still it was of consequence, if we could manage it, to possess ourselves of the Indians' bows and spears. I again offered to accompany the trapper. He thought a moment.

" It may be done," he said, " if you step cautiously, for they are more soundly asleep than I had supposed ; but, if any of them should awake, you must be prepared to knock them on the head—our own safety will demand it."

I agreed to this, hoping that the contingency might not arrive. We set out and soon reached the camp. So sound asleep did they appear, that I believe even had we trodden on them, they could not have been aroused. They lay where they had fallen in their drunken fits, in every variety of attitude. We each possessed ourselves of two tomahawks for our defence, and all the bows we could find; and, carrying them under our arms, returned to our companions. Folkard immediately cut the strings and broke off the ends of the bows. We had thus far been more successful than we had anticipated.

We now, having recovered our weapons and two

"THEY SEEMED TO BE SEIZED BY A SUDDEN PANIC." [*p.* 157.

saddles,—for the Indians had left the others on the backs of the horses,—glided behind the trees to which we had been bound, and stole off, cautiously following the footsteps of old Folkard, who led the way.

"I left my horse down in the hollow yonder," said the trapper; "we will get him first, and then I'll try and help catch yours; they are not far off I suspect. It will be daylight soon, and we have no time to lose."

Several more minutes were spent before we reached the spot where old Folkard's horse was securely tethered. He having mounted, we set out in search of our own steeds.

"It is just possible that the Indians may have left one of their number to watch their horses as well as ours, and if so, it will be necessary to either capture or kill the man," said Dick.

Unwilling as we were to put to death any of our savage enemies, even in our own defence, we saw the necessity of doing as Dick proposed.

Greatly to our satisfaction, as we approached a glade, the whinny of a horse was heard, and Armitage's favourite steed came trotting up to him. We immediately put on its saddle and bridle. Pierre's and mine were still wanting. His had probably been torn to pieces by the wolves, but we still had a chance of getting mine. I was almost in despair, when to my joy it came up, and I was quickly on its back. Pierre was very unhappy at delaying us.

At length old Folkard observed—

"Jump up behind me, we'll soon catch a horse for

you; the Indians had a lot of animals with them, and we'll take one of theirs if we can't find yours."

By this time morning had dawned, and we had no longer any fear of encountering our enemies. We rode on to where old Folkard told us he expected to find the horses.

Surmounting a slight elevation, we soon caught sight of a score of animals, evidently those of the Indians. To catch them was no easy matter, for just at the moment we appeared they seemed to be seized by a sudden panic, and began prancing and rearing in the strangest fashion. We dashed forward, and, as they saw us coming, off they started across the prairie at a rate which would have rendered pursuit utterly hopeless.

We had now to settle what course to pursue. Should we return to the camp and take possession of our property, or put as many miles as we could between ourselves and the Indians?

On calculating, however, the quantity of liquor among our stores, we arrived at the conclusion that there was enough to keep the Indians drunk for another day or two, and that we should probably find them as helpless as before. We accordingly kept our rifles ready for instant service, and rode towards our camp. On our way we found our mules, which according to their usual custom had not mixed with the horses. Pierre mounted one of them, and led the rest. The loud snores and perfect silence around where the Indians lay showed us that they had not recovered from their debauch. While two of our party stood guard, ready to deal with any who might come to their senses, the rest of us loaded the mules with our goods, including two remaining bottles of spirits.

Folkard proposed leaving these to prevent the enemy from pursuing us. "There is no fear of their doing that, for they have neither horses nor arms," observed Dick. "They may consider themselves fortunate in escaping with their lives." We could scarcely help laughing at the thought of their astonishment when, on coming to themselves, they should find how completely the tables had been turned: we hoped they would duly appreciate the mercy shown to them. We now rode off, thankful for the happy termination of our adventure.

We found that the old trapper had been very successful and wished to turn his steps eastward.

"I should be glad of your company, friends," he said, "in the first place; and in the second I don't think it would be safe for you to remain in this region, as the rest of the tribe may consider themselves insulted, and, ungrateful for the mercy shown their people, may endeavour to cut you off. When the Redskins have made up their minds to do a thing, they'll do it if they can, however long they may have to wait."

We all agreed that, although not frightened by the Indians, we had had enough of fighting and hunting for the present. We accordingly made up our minds to accompany old Folkard. We felt that, in gratitude to him for having preserved our lives, we were bound to do as he wished.

Having reached the spot where he had left his

mules with his traps and peltries, we turned our horses' heads eastward. As we rode along he told us that he had come upon our trail, and that soon afterwards he had fallen in with one which he knew must be made by an Indian war-party, and feeling sure that they intended us mischief he had followed them up. He had scarcely expected, however, to find us still alive; but having stolen up to the camp, he saw the state to which our liquor had fortunately reduced our captors, and had at once formed the plan for liberating us so happily carried out. One of Dick's first questions was about Charley. The old trapper replied that he had failed to hear of him ; but he still held out hopes that our friend might have escaped, and that some well-disposed Indians might have spared his life, and taken care of him, hoping to induce him to join their tribe, according to a by no means unusual custom among them.

This idea somewhat cheered up the worthy lieu-tenant's spirits, and made him unwilling to return eastward ; still, as he could not remain by himself, he agreed to accompany us. The journey appeared very long. For the first few days we pushed forward to get beyond the reach of the Indians, in case they should fall in with any of their tribe and venture to pursue us. After this we were compelled, for the sake of our horses, to make more easy stages. We had also to halt for the purpose of providing ourselves with meat; but as we shot only for the pot, that caused us no great delay.

At last we reached St. Louis, where we spent several months enjoying the hospitality of numerous friends to whom we had letters of introduction. For a time we were looked upon as heroes on a small scale by society; but probably the hunters and trappers who frequent that city would have considered our adventures as every-day occurrences and scarcely worth talking about.

Old Folkard, having disposed of his peltries, and obtained new traps and a fresh outfit, started westward in the course of a fortnight, declaring that he could not breathe among the bricks and mortar. He promised that he would not fail to look out for Charley, for whose recovery, however, even Dick, by this time, had begun to despair. We were beginning to get a little tired of civilised ways and to sigh for the wild life of the prairie, when Armitage received a letter calling him to New York to meet an agent.

"I should like to continue the expedition I began with you," he said, " and I shall esteem it a favour if you will wait for my return; I shall not be longer than I can help."

His request, made in so courteous a way, was not to be refused. We all consented to stop. Week after week went by, and Armitage was still delayed; but as we had remained so long, we agreed to wait until he returned, though our stay was double the length we intended. We were employed in adding to our outfit such articles as, from our experience, we considered useful. At length Armitage rejoined us, and we were once more *en route.* From the way his Indians had behaved when it came to a pinch, he had resolved to take no more. Besides Pierre, who was accompanied by another Canadian, we had a Yankee

trapper yclept "Long Sam," who, according to his
own showing, was likely to prove of far more value
than half-a-dozen Indians. He was ready for anything—to hunt on horseback, to shoot on foot, or to
trap beavers. We had been travelling on some time
when Armitage began to talk of Tillydrone, and suggested that, as it was not far out of our way, it would
be but courteous to pay a visit there and inquire after
the family who had treated us so hospitably. He
said not a word, however, about Miss Hargrave, nor
from the tone of his voice would anyone have suspected
that he was thinking of her.

When Long Sam heard us mention the place, he
exclaimed—

"Why, that's wha'r Praeger used to live, and it
was burnt with mighty near the whole of the property when the forest caught fire last fall, though he
and his family escaped. I heard say that they were
going to move westward, and they must be on their
journey by this time, I guess."

Armitage questioned and cross-questioned his in-
formant, and seemed perfectly satisfied with his
statement. After this he expressed no further wish
to visit Tillydrone.

We had been travelling on for more than a month,
when we once more found ourselves among the wild
and grand scenery in the neighbourhood of the
Rocky Mountains. We encamped not far from a
spot we had before occupied, where we knew an
abundance of game was to be found. This time we
had determined that nothing should turn us back
until the western coast was reached. We were now

enabled to detect the trails of animals as well as of men, an art indeed in which Pierre and Sam were equal to the Indians themselves. As we had camped pretty early, we started in different directions, hoping to bring in a good supply of meat, of which our consumption was considerable, Long Sam declaring when really hungry, that he could eat half a buffalo at a sitting—I wonder he didn't say a whole one. We had espied some big-horns on the rocky heights in the distance, and were making our way towards them, when Sam exclaimed—

" A white man has passed this way, though those are the marks of moccasins, but no Indian treads in that fashion."

I agreed with him, and soon afterwards we came upon a pool out of which a stream ran to the eastward. Sam was not long before he ferreted out several beaver-traps, and, examining one of them, pronounced it of the best make, and belonging to a white trapper. Of course we allowed it to remain unchanged. We thought of old Folkard, but scarcely expected to fall in with him again. We were making our way through a wood, along a ridge with a valley below us, when, looking through a gap in the trees, I caught sight of two persons, the one seated, supporting the head of another, who was stretched on the ground on his knees. Though I was too far off to distinguish their features, I saw by the dress of one that he was a trapper, but could not make out the other. On coming nearer, however, I recognized old Folkard; but who was the other? His cheeks were hollow, his countenance haggard, and, though

CHARLEY AND HIS NURSE.

sunburnt, showed none of the hue of health. A
second glance, however, convinced me that he was
Charley Fielding. The old hunter was engaged in
giving him some food, treating him as he would a
helpless child. They both recognized me, and
Charley's eye brightened as he stretched out his
hand to welcome me while I knelt by his side.

"Where have you been? How did you come
here?" I asked eagerly.

"Don't trouble him with questions," said the old
trapper; "he'll answer you better when he's had
some broth. I found him not long since pretty well
at his last gasp. I guess he has got away from
some Redskins. I always said he was carried off
by them. If I am right they are not likely to be
far away. We must be on the look-out not to be
caught by them."

Charley, though unable to speak, showed by the
expression of his countenance that the old trapper
had truly conjectured what had happened.

We naturally, forgetting all about the big-horns,
thought only of how we could best convey Charley
to the camp. As we had come over some exces-
sively rough ground, it would be no easy matter to
get him there.

"Then go back to your friends, and get them to
move camp up here," said the trapper; "by keeping along the lower ground, they can be here
quickly, and it's a more secure spot, I guess, than
where they are."

I asked Long Sam, who now came up, to go
back with a message to our friends, as I was un-

willing to leave Charley. This he agreed to do, and Folkard was glad to have me remain. The food quickly revived Charley, when Folkard went off to fetch some water from a neighbouring spring. We then together carried him to the trapper's camp, which was not many paces off, though so securely hidden that even an Indian's eye could scarcely have detected it.

This done, I looked out anxiously for the arrival of our friends. The shades of evening were already extending far away over the lower ground.

"They'll surely come!" I said to myself. Presently I caught sight of our party, and shouted to them to come on.

Poor Dick burst into tears when he saw Charley, partly from joy at having found him, and partly from pity at his condition.

It was some time before Charley could speak. The first use he made of his returning strength, was to tell us that he had been captured by Indians, and kept a prisoner ever since,—exactly as old Folkard had supposed; that he was not as badly treated as he expected, but so strictly watched, that in spite of all the attempts he had made, he could not effect his escape until two days before, when he found that a war-party was about to set off to attack an emigrant train coming westward, of which they had just gained tidings. While the braves were performing their war-dance to the admiration of the squaws, he had managed to slip out of camp unperceived, his intention being to warn the white men of their danger. The train had been encamped some days, and it was not known how soon they would move forward. He had hoped therefore to be in time, as the Indians would not venture to attack them while they remained stationary.

On hearing this we were all eager to set out to the rescue of the white people. Armitage especially was unusually excited, but to move at that time of night, with our horses already tired, the country also being of a somewhat rough description, was scarcely possible. Old Folkard, as well as Pierre and Long Sam, was of opinion that we should gain time by waiting, as we might otherwise lose our way, or lame our animals over the rocky tract we should have to pass. We arranged therefore to wait for daylight, and it was settled that the Canadian should remain with the old trapper to assist him in taking care of Charley, and looking after our baggage mules and spare horses. The greater part of the night was spent in cleaning our rifles and pistols, as we expected to have use for them should we find that the emigrant train had moved on, and that the Indians had kept up their intention of attacking it. We breakfasted before dawn so that we might ride if necessary several hours without food, and might be some distance on our way before the first streaks of the coming day should appear in the sky.

Pierre and Long Sam, after a consultation, undertook to guide us, so that we might fall in with the usual track followed by emigrants, a short distance only to the northward of the place where we were encamped. We felt somewhat anxious about leaving Charley in his present state, with so slender a guard

"Do not trouble yourselves about that," observed the old trapper. "I'll keep a good look-out, and no Redskins are likely to come this way."

As we rode on and daylight increased, we looked out eagerly for any smoke which might indicate a camp fire, but not the slightest wreath dimmed the clear sky. Pierre and Long Sam both agreed that we were not far from the high road, and that we must soon come upon the track of the train if it had passed. Not a quarter-of-an-hour after this, we saw —not a fire burning—but the remains of several, and all the signs of a train having halted on the spot. We hastily rode over the ground, when Armitage, suddenly leaping from his horse, picked up a small object which he intently examined. It was a lady's glove, such as the usual travellers by emigrant trains are not wont to wear. He placed it in his pocket.

"On, friends, on!" he cried; "if Charley's information is correct we have not a moment to lose. Already the work of plunder and murder may have begun."

We needed no further incitement to make us urge on our steeds. Armitage and Long Sam, who were the best mounted of our party, leading, the latter being our guide. The country was wooded so that we could not see far ahead. Suddenly our guide turned to the left.

"We will take a short cut for the waggons. The road makes a bend here," he observed. "Maybe we shall find ourselves in front of the train. No Redskins will venture to attack it when they see us."

No sounds had hitherto reached our ears, but presently a shot was heard from a short distance off, then another and another.

"On, on!" cried Armitage, and in a few minutes, through an opening in the forest, we caught sight of a large band of Indians rapidly descending the hill, while nearer to us there came the leading waggon of an emigrant train, the drivers of which were endeavouring to turn back their cattle as probably those following were attempting to do.

From the shrieks and cries which arose, it seemed too likely that the Redskins had already attacked the travellers, and we knew well what quick work they would make of it should they have gained any advantage; so, digging spurs into our horses' flanks, we passed round the head of the train, and uttering a loud cheer as we did so to encourage the emigrants, we rode full tilt at the savages.

CHAPTER IX.

As we rode round the head of the train, we saw to our sorrow that the Redskins had already fought their way to two of the centre waggons, the white men belonging to which were engaged in a fierce fight with them. Armitage took an anxious glance at the occupants of the leading waggon.

"Who commands this train?" he asked eagerly of one of the drivers.

The man, owing to the war-whoops of the savages, the shrieks of the women, and the shouts of his companion, did not perhaps hear the question, and there was no time to repeat it as we swooped by. Already it appeared to us that the work of murder had commenced. Two or three of the people lay on the ground, and while part of the Indians were fighting, some were engaged in attempting to drag off the female occupants of the waggon. To prevent them succeeding in their desperate attempt was our first object. Leaving the Indians we had intended to charge, we turned our horses and dashed forward towards the point where our services were most required. The savages saw us coming, and most of them leaving the waggon, some leapt on their horses, while others attempted to defend themselves on foot. Firing a volley from our rifles which brought several to the ground, we rushed at our foes. Just then I saw, to my horror, an Indian, who by his dress appeared to be a chief, dragging off a female, a fair girl she seemed, whom he lifted on his horse. In vain she struggled to free herself. He was mounted on a powerful animal which he evidently had under perfect command. Shouting to his followers he galloped off, while they stood their ground boldly. We dashed at them pistoling some and cutting down others; but not until half their number lay dead on the ground or desperately wounded did they attempt to escape; by which time the main body were almost up to us. Leaving the first to be dealt with by the emigrants who had rallied, we reloaded our rifles and charged the larger party of the enemy. They received us with a shower of arrows, by which, wonderful as it seemed, none of us were wounded. The odds, however, were fearfully against us; for the Indians fought bravely, and rapidly wheeling their horses attacked us now in front, now on our flanks, and we had to turn every instant to defend ourselves. Several of their number had been shot. Dick and Armitage were wounded, and Pierre's horse was killed. It was with the greatest difficulty that we defended him until he managed to make his escape towards the waggons. I shouted to him to send some of the men to our assistance. We in the meantime having fired our rifles and pistols had our swords alone to depend upon. They served us well,

and the Indians, as we approached, evidently showed
their dread of them by endeavouring to get out of
their reach as we flashed them round our heads.
Still, numbers might prevail, unless we could speedily
compel the Indians to take to flight.

In the meantime, what had become of the female
I had seen carried off! I could not tell whether
Armitage or the rest had witnessed the occurrence;
but, whether or not, it would be impossible to attempt
her rescue until we had defeated our present opponents. If we could have retreated even to a short
distance to reload our firearms, we would have done
so, but our agile foes gave us no time. I scarcely
even dared to look round to ascertain if any help was
coming; probably the emigrants had enough to do
in keeping in check other parties of Indians who were
threatening them. The fight had not continued
many minutes, though it seemed to me as many
hours, when an Indian charged at Armitage with a
long spear, the weapon pierced his side, and over
rolled horse and man. Another savage was coming
on to repeat the blow, when Long Sam, dashing up,
cut down the first savage, and then engaged the
second. Our friend, notwithstanding, would speedily
have been killed, had we not rallied round him and
kept the enemy at bay; while, although evidently
much hurt, he managed to regain his feet.

Now deprived of two of our number, and having to
defend Armitage as well as ourselves, we were nearly
overpowered. At any moment another of us might
be wounded. The Indians, seeing their advantage,
retreated to a short distance, in order to make

"A STRANGE FIGURE DASHED BY US." p. 175

another fierce charge, the result of which would very probably have been our overthrow, when we heard a loud shout raised in our rear, and presently, with a wild war-cry of "Erin go bragh," a strange figure dashed by us, mounted on a powerful horse, with a target on one arm, and a broadsword flashing in his right hand. Several arrows were shot at him, but he caught them on his target, and dashed on unharmed. The first Indian he attacked bit the dust; another made at him, the head of whose spear he lopped off with a single blow, and he then clove his opponent from the crown of the head to the neck. On seeing this, the Indians, crying out to each other, turned their horses' heads and attempted to escape.

Their flight was expedited by several of the emigrants who, brought up by Pierre, fired a volley at them as they retreated. On looking at the old warrior who had come so opportunely to our aid, what was my surprise to recognize Ben Folkard.

The diversion thus made in our favour, had enabled the emigrants to form their waggons into a square, so as to be able to repel any further attacks of the Indians, who showed no disposition however to come on. Our first care was to commit Armitage—the most severely wounded of our party—to the charge of Pierre and the emigrants who had accompanied him. Lifting him up between them, they carried him to the waggons.

"I'm main sure that Mr. Praeger will be grateful to the gentlemen," I heard one of the men say.

As the man uttered the name, the thought flashed across me, " Could it have been one of his daughters, or Miss Hargrave, I had seen carried off? Poor Armitage, how fearful would be his feelings should he find that his Ellen had disappeared. As soon as I could, I turned to the old trapper and anxiously inquired what had become of Charley."

"I left him in safe keeping," he answered, "but, finding from a companion of mine who rejoined me after you had gone that the Indians were about to attack the train in greater force than I had at first supposed, I resolved to come to your assistance."

"You did well," observed Dick, who came up while he was speaking. "Had it not been for your arrival, I suspect that one and all of us would have gone down, for those rascals pressed us hard."

We had been proceeding towards a height which commanded a view in the direction our late opponents were supposed to have taken, and we were thankful to see them moving off, forming a more numerous body than we had at first supposed. We accounted for this by concluding that, while one portion of the savages attacked the train, the others had remained concealed to act as a reserve should the first not succeed. What had become of the female I had seen carried off, we could not ascertain. We could nowhere distinguish her, but she might easily have been concealed from our sight if she were among the leading Indians.

Our party, however, was too small to pursue the fugitives, with any chance of recovering her. On reaching the camp formed by the train, we at once repaired to Mr. Praeger's waggon. We found him and his family almost overcome with grief and anxiety. Two of his sons were severely wounded, and Miss Hargrave had disappeared. My worst fears were realized. She must have been the person I had seen carried off by the Indian chief.

No one was certain as to the direction her captor had taken, for his followers immediately surrounded him, and they had retreated together. Three men of the emigrant party had been killed, and half a dozen more or less wounded. They were full of gratitude to us for coming to their assistance; for they acknowledged, surprised as they had been, that every one of them might have been massacred had we not attacked the savages. We on our part had to thank the trapper for his assistance. When, however, we looked round for him, he had disappeared, and some of the people said they had seen him galloping back in the direction from which he had come. We guessed therefore that he had returned to take care of our friend Charley. Poor Armitage had been placed in one of the waggons, and a surgeon who had accompanied the train was attending to his wounds. He had not been told of what had happened to Miss Hargrave.

We had now to consider what was next to be done. Of course we all agreed that the first thing was to endeavour to recover the young lady. The leaders of the train, in consequence of having so many wounded among them, resolved to remain encamped where they were, as the neighbourhood afforded wood and water, with abundance of game, and they felt pretty confident that the Indians would not again venture to attack them. Pierre and Long Sam at once volunteered to visit old Folkard's camp, and to assist in

N

bringing on Charley, should he, as we hoped would be the case, be in a fit state to be moved. They also promised to consult the trapper, as his experience would be of value in forming a plan for the recovery of the young lady : that she had been killed, we none of us could bring ourselves to believe.

All hands were now employed in strengthening the camp,—Dick, Story, and I, assisted our friends, working as hard as any one. We were of use also in attending to poor Armitage. I was afraid every moment that he would inquire for Miss Hargrave, for he would naturally wonder that she had not appeared.

As may be supposed, we kept a very strict watch at night, while all the men lay down with their arms by their sides under the waggons, with the cattle placed in the centre of the square; but no Indians, we believed, came near us.

As the morning advanced, I looked out eagerly for the arrival of Charley. We were anxious to place him under the protection of our friends, and until Pierre and Long Sam came, we could take no steps for the recovery of Miss Hargrave. We talked the subject over with Mr. Praeger, who was naturally too much agitated to be able with sufficient calmness to design any feasible plan of operation.

At length, greatly to our relief, soon after mid-day Pierre and Long Sam appeared with two other men, carrying Charley on a litter; while old Folkard and another trapper followed, leading the horses and laden mules. Charley was much revived, and declared that he could have walked had his companions allowed him; but when he came to be placed on his feet, it was very evident that he could not have pro-ceeded many yards by himself.

No time was lost in holding a council round the camp fire, while the new arrivals ate the dinner pro-vided for them. Old Folkard advised that we should in the first place examine the neighbourhood of the camp, in order to try and discover the trail of Miss Hargrave's captor, for Long Sam was of opinion that, though he might have been accompanied by a few of his braves, he had not gone off with the larger body of Redskins. Charley, who listened attentively to all that was said, agreed with Long Sam; and, as he had been so long amongst the tribe, his opinion was of value. He was certain that it was only a chief who was likely to have committed such an act, probably the younger brother of the head chief; who, Charley said, had frequently talked to him of the beauty of the pale faced women, and of his intention of obtaining one of them for his wife. This had always greatly angered his elder brother, who had declared, should he bring a pale-face to their lodges, that he should be turned out of the tribe, and that she should be put to death. Charley was certain, therefore, that Black Eagle—so the chief was called—would not return to his people; and that, should we be able to dis-cover his trail, we should find him protected with only a small band, with whom it would not be diffi-cult to deal.

The first thing was to discover the trail, and Folkard, Long Sam, and Pierre set out for the pur-pose. We, in the meantime, were engaged in organizing the pursuing party, if so I may call it. Dick, though wounded, made light of the matter, and insisted on going. Folkard had offered to take all his people. Besides Story and I, we had Pierre, and Long Sam, the Canadian, and two other men ; making altogether a well-armed party of twelve, mostly experienced hunters and backwoodsmen, accustomed all their lives to encounters with the red men.

Long Sam, who in his wanderings in South America had learned the use of the lasso, never went on an expedition without carrying a long coil of rope at his saddle bow ; which he used, not only for catching horses, but for stopping the career of a wounded buffalo or deer; and he had, he asserted, made captives at different times of several Indians by whom he had been attacked, when they, approaching within the radius of his long line, were surprised to find themselves jerked to the ground and dragged along at a rate which rendered all resistance useless.

It was late in the evening when the three trappers returned. They had discovered a trail made by a small party, though they had been unable to decide whether it was that which had carried off the lady, until Long Sam, observing an object glittering on the ground, had, on picking it up, found it to be a golden locket, such as was not likely to have belonged to an Indian. On showing it to Mr. Praeger and his family, they at once recognized it as having been worn by Miss Hargrave, thus leaving us in no doubt on the subject.

It was too late that night to follow up the trail, though every moment was precious. We had to wait,

BLACK EAGLE LASSOED. [p. 184

therefore, until about three hours before dawn; when, mounting our steeds, we rode forward under the guidance of old Folkard, expecting at daybreak to reach the spot where the locket had been found. We agreed to breakfast there, and then to follow up the trail as soon as there was sufficient light to see it.

We carried out our plan, and the rising sun saw us pushing eagerly forward, the trail being sufficiently marked to enable the practical eyes of our guides to detect it.

To our surprise, instead of keeping to the right, as both old Folkard and Long Sam expected, it turned suddenly to the left, in the direction the main body had taken.

" There's a reason for this," observed Folkard, after we had ridden some way. " See, there was a message sent by the head chief to Black Eagle. Look, there is the trail of his horse, but whether the young chief joined the main body we shall know by and by."

This information was a great disappointment, as it would render our enterprise far more difficult, for we should now have the whole tribe to deal with instead of a small party as we expected.

We were not to be deterred, however, and rode forward as rapidly as the necessary examination of the trail would allow. At last we had to halt and rest our horses, but we refrained from lighting a fire and ate our provisions cold.

As soon as possible we again pushed forward, but darkness coming on we had again to camp. Of course we did not light a fire, lest, should our enemies be in the neighbourhood, they might discover us.

Our faithful attendants kept watch, insisting that Story and I should lie down and take the rest we so greatly needed.

Next morning, instead of riding on together, Long Sam undertook to scout in advance, that we might not come suddenly upon the enemy, who it was believed could not be far ahead. We were passing round a wood when presently we heard a shout, and directly afterwards caught sight of Long Sam galloping towards us followed by an Indian—evidently a chief, from his war plumes and gaily bedecked shield, —but as we got nearer we saw that a rope was round the Indian's body, and that he was attempting to free himself from it. He was on the point of drawing his knife when, by a sudden jerk, Long Sam brought him to the ground.

Folkard and Pierre, throwing themselves from their horses, rushed forward to seize him before he had regained his feet. Pierre, with his knife in his hand, was about to plunge it into the heart of the Indian; but I shouted out to him to desist, and Long Sam drawing tight the lasso, the next instant dragged the Indian clear of his frightened steed, which galloped off leaving him utterly helpless. Springing upon him, we then secured his arms by some leathern thongs, and removed the lasso from round his body.

"He is Black Eagle, no doubt about that," cried old Folkard. "What have you done with the lady you carried off?" he added in the Indian tongue.

The prisoner refused to reply.

" If the chief will tell us what we want to know, he shall live; but, if not, he must be prepared to die," said Long Sam.

An expression of irresolution passed over the Indian's countenance.

" I would that I could tell the pale-faces where she is to be found, but she has been taken from me; though, if they will restore me to liberty, I will endeavour to find her," he said at length.

" If the chief speaks the truth, he will find the pale-faces willing to grant him any favour he may ask," said Long Sam; then, turning to us, he added, " We must not trust the rascal. Though decked with fine feathers he has a cowardly heart, I suspect. We'll keep him bound and take him with us. If he plays us false, knock him on the head without scruple ; that's my advice. We must not let his horse escape, however; wait here while I catch the animal."

Saying this, Long Sam threw himself into the saddle, and taking his lasso which he had again coiled up, started off in the direction the Indian's horse had taken. In a shorter time than I had expected, he returned leading the animal by the lasso which he had thrown over its neck, and whenever it became restive, a sudden jerk quickly brought it again under subjection.

" Of course, it won't do to put the Redskin on his own horse, or he may be giving us the slip. He shall have mine," said Long Sam, " and old 'Knotty' will stick by us, even if Mr. Black Eagle should try and gallop off."

We now, by means of the three hunters, endeavoured to obtain all the information we could from
our captive.

He acknowledged that he had carried off the pale-
faced girl, and that he intended to make her his
bride; but that he had been inveigled into the camp
of his people, when she had been taken from him;
and that, when he complained, he had been turned
away to seek his own fortunes.

As we had no reason to doubt his word we asked
him to guide us to wherever his people were now
encamped, making him promise to warn us as we
drew near the spot so that we might not be taken
by surprise. We kept a bright look out on Black
Eagle, Long Sam hinting gently that, should he
show any treachery, he would be immediately shot
through the head. The warning was not lost upon
our friend. We rode on and on, until the sun
sinking in the west showed us that we must again
camp.

Black Eagle informed us that we should probably
not reach his people until late on the following day.
We had therefore to restrain our anxiety, and trust
to his assurances that there were no Indians in the
neighbourhood. We lighted a fire to cook a deer
which Long Sam had shot just before we reached the
camp.

We were seated round the fire enjoying our
suppers, the first satisfactory meal we had taken
since we started, when the well-known cry of a pack
of wolves reached our ears. From the yelps and
barks which they continued to utter in full chorus,

we knew that they were in chase of some unfortunate animal which they hoped to drag to the ground.

The sounds grew nearer and nearer, but as the spot where we were encamped was surrounded with rocks and trees we could not see to any distance. At last Dick jumped up, saying he must have a look at the wolves and the animal they were chasing. Story and I quickly followed.

" They are not worth powder and shot," observed Long Sam, but notwithstanding he came after us, as did indeed the whole party.

Just then the moon rose behind the cliffs, shedding a bright light over the rocky ground which surrounded the spot. From where we stood, we could see an animal, apparently a horse, dashing on at full speed with a savage pack of llovo wolves close at its heels. The next instant, as it came bounding on over the rocks, what was our horror to observe a female form lashed to its back.

To stop it in its mad career seemed impossible. The only hope was to shoot some of the wolves, and thus give a better chance for the escape of the horse. As I fired, I heard several other shots, and saw that most of the brutes, already at the horse's heels, were rolled over. Still the condition of the female was perilous in the extreme. Unless we could catch our own horses, and overtake the affrighted steed, her destruction appeared inevitable. Scarcely had this thought flashed across my mind, when I saw Long Sam, who had thrown himself on horseback, galloping along with his lasso to intercept the runaway.

I ran as I had never run before, regardless of the wolves, in the same direction.   As I passed by I saw that the **pack** had stopped and were already engaged in tearing to pieces the brutes we had shot. In an instant afterwards, it seemed, I observed Long Sam's lasso cast with unerring aim over the neck of the frantic steed, which plunged and reared, but happily did not fall over.   In another moment Sam had drawn the lasso so tightly round its neck that it was unable to move.

We sprang forward, cut the thongs which bound the female to the animal's back, and lifting her to the ground, carried her out of danger.   She still breathed, though apparently perfectly unconscious. The light of the moon showed us the features of Ellen Hargrave.

We did not stop to see what Long Sam did with the captured horse, but at once carried the young lady to the camp, when, by sprinkling her face with water and bathing her hands, she in a short time was restored to consciousness.

Her first impulse was to return thanks to heaven for her preservation.   Looking up she recognised Dick and me.

"Where is Harry?   Where is Mr. Armitage?" she asked, evidently concluding that he must be of our-party.

Dick replied that he was safe in the camp with her friends; that we had beaten the savages who had attacked them, and, finding that she had been carried off, had come in search of her.   Though we did not inquire how she had been treated in

MISS HARGRAVE IN PERIL

the Indian camp, she without hesitation told uɪ
that Black Eagle had been compelled to release heɪ
by his superior chief ; when, having been kept in
a wigwam by herself for some hours, she had been
bound to a horse, which being led away from the
camp had been driven out into the wilds. She was
fully prepared, she said, for a lingering death, but
still she prayed that she might be preserved. All
hope however had gone when she heard in the distance the howls of the wolves, and the horse sprang
forward on its mad career over the rocky ground.
" The rest you know," she added. "I would thank-
fully forget those fearful moments."

I must make a long story short. Miss Hargrave
appeared much recovered after a night's rest in the
hut we built for her, and the next morning we formed
a litter on which we carried her a day's journey ; but
on the following morning she insisted on mounting
one of the horses, and, a side-saddle being prepared,
she performed the rest of the distance to camp with
out apparent suffering.

I need not say that she was received by her relatives as one returned from the dead, while they
expressed their gratitude to us by every means in
their power. Armitage, they stated, had been in a
very precarious state, but he revived on seeing Miss
Hargrave, and quickly regained his strength. We
allowed the Black Eagle to go free with his horse
and arms, he promising, in return for the merciful
treatment he had received, that he would in future be
the friend of the pale-faces. The wounded men
having now recovered sufficiently to travel, camp

was struck, and the train continued its course westward.

We, of course, felt ourselves in honour bound to escort our friends on their way ; and, although we at first talked of leaving them as soon as all fear of an attack from the Indians had passed, we continued on from day to day.

Before the journey was over, it was generally known that Armitage was to marry Miss Hargrave, while Dick and Story, though supposed to be confirmed bachelors, lost their hearts to the two youngest Miss Praegers ; and a very pleasant wedding it was which took place soon after our arrival at Mr. Praeger's new location. We frequently afterwards met in old England, where my friends took their wives, and many a long yarn was spun about our adventures in the wild regions of the " Far West."

THE END.

BRADBURY, AGNEW, & CO. LIMD., PRINTERS, WHITEFRIARS

www.ingramcontent.com/pod-product-compliance
Lightning Source LLC
Chambersburg PA
CBHW030555040726
47497CB00008B/2732